WAHIDA CLARK INNOVATIVE PUBLISHING

COVID, MAYHEM AND MURDER

A HEADHUNTERS CHRISTMAS

BY WAHIDA CLARK

Wahida Clark Presents Publishing
60 Evergreen Place Suite 904
East Orange, NJ 07018

www.wclarkpublishing.com

email: info@wclarkpublishing.com

Copyright 2020 © by Wahida Clark

COVID, MAYHEN AND MURDER: A HEADHUNTERS CHRISTMAS

ISBN 13-digit 978-1-954161-14-6 (Paperback)
ISBN 13-digit 978-1-954161-15-3 (Hardback)
ISBN 13-digit 978-1-954161-13-9 (E-book)

1. Covid-19   2. Coronavirus Pandemic
3. Pandemic   4. Quarantine
5. Lockdown   6. Murder
7. Home Invasion   8. Social Media
9. Masks   10. Holiday

nuanceart@acreativenuance.com

Printed in United States

COVID, MAYHEM AND MURDER

A HEADHUNTERS CHRISTMAS

Backcover Synopsis

MARCO IS A HUSTLER'S HUSTLER. Loyalty proves more than a word when his plug, Genesis, commands him to kill a traitor in his Atlanta-based crew during the Christmas season. Marco agrees because he is willing to do anything to carve out a place as Genesis' right hand. But when top-level hustlers in Genesis' camp start turning up dead from the result of a string of robberies in the midst of the coronavirus pandemic, Marco must discover who the robbers are, and deal with them, before his head ends up on a plate. But the deeper he digs, the more he realizes that these unique robbers are not what most people would suspect.

Haunted by their mother's murder nearly a decade ago sisters Rochelle and Lacy struggle to find their way in life. Despite a tremendous amount of pressure from her sister to go to college Lacy instead finds comfort in the streets. As her sister hustles to keep a roof over their head, Lacy thinks the double life she's living is being kept secret, but soon realizes that she and her sister Rochelle have much more in common than they know.

Dedication

I hope you all enjoy this Street Lit Christmas Story that was written during covid, inspired by covid. Please stay safe and much love.

Your Number #Cheerleader

Wahida Clark

The Official Queen of Street Lit

P.S. Team WCP you guys are the best of the best.

Contents

ONE 1

TWO 10

THREE 24

FOUR 34

FIVE 43

SIX 55

SEVEN 65

EIGHT 76

NINE 84

TEN 91

ELEVEN 100

TWELVE 111

THIRTEEN 123

FOURTEEN 131

FIFTEEN 140

SIXTEEN 149

SEVENTEEN 155

EIGHTEEN 164

NINETEEN 174

TWENTY 183

TWENTY ONE 190

TWENTY TWO 198

TWENTY THREE..203

TWENTY FOUR 212

TWENTY FIVE 218

TWENTY SIX 224

TWENTY SEVEN 229

EPILOGUE: GENESIS RISING 234

ONE

THE HOUSE SAT AT THE BOTTOM of a steep hill on Mill Lake Circle in the Memorial Plantation neighborhood in Stone Mountain, Georgia. Though the front of the house was bathed in shadows the two dark figures hustling down the street knew someone was home. Both were dressed in all black. Both wore black hospital masks to conceal their face and nose. The one with lighter skin wore a black toboggan. The other, darker one, wore a green Grinch hat that had a white ball dangling from the top. They knelt beside a black Nissan Maxima that was parked in the house's driveway. Its twenty-inch chrome rims sparkled in the dim porch light.

An occupied house raised the level of danger. There could be a gun in that house. Someone could die tonight. Yet they stalked the suburban home like big cats on the hunt, with their mouths watering for a meal. The danger did not outweigh the rewards. What they were about to do was not much different than lions, tigers or panthers hunting for sustenance. The commonality was the basic principle of survival. No one considered a savage beast a murderer when it killed to eat. It was the same for the masked figures. They were robbing to survive the tragedy of being trapped in lower-income lives they could not escape, where the odds of the world were stacked against them.

It was well after two that cold December morning. Adrenaline charged their veins as they hurried away from the side of the car to the side of the house. Nothing more. Their hot breath—blocked by the facemasks they wore—ballooned out in misty clouds in their wake.

Most windows of the surrounding houses were black beyond their glass facades, letting the masked goons know that if anyone was home, they were in a dead sleep. The only lights on the street were the colored Christmas lights framing some windows. But, most homes donned no holiday lights. It didn't mean that they didn't celebrate Christmas, most likely they were just too poor to buy lights. Many people in the ghetto couldn't afford Christmas cheer, especially now during the coronavirus pandemic when many families are struggling to put food on the table. Cheer was the last emotion most in the Memorial Plantation subdivision felt.

The figures paused on the side of the house. Their target had no Christmas lights illuminating the night, providing a shadow where the goons could perch without being seen. The first figure hugged the wall, gripping a rusty twenty-two low against the thigh in a leather-gloved hand. The handle had been wrapped in duct tape by its previous owner. The safety didn't work. They could only squeeze three bullets into the clip, not the seven it was designed to hold. It was the only pistol they had, but it would do the trick. The second figure slipped in beside the first, pressing a slim finger to the black face covering where lips should be. The first figure nodded and tensed an index finger around the trigger. They both looked toward a tall wooden fence bordering the house's backyard.

They scampered in a stooped crouch across the short patch of dirt that was supposed to be a lawn.

The fence leading to the backyard proved easy to scale. They made it over and tiptoed to the sliding glass door at the back of the house. The long, vertical blinds waved with the warm air blowing from the heater inside the house. The dark-skinned goon peeked in and spotted no moving figures, then reached out and tried the door. It was still unlocked, as they had left it the night before. It slid open as silently as words whispered in the wind.

The house was warm and comfortable when they entered. The brown-skinned goon directed the way, leading with the gun in case someone surprised them. They stood just inside the door for a moment, allowing their eyes to adjust to the darkness of the house. Then they took tentative steps through the kitchen, down the hall, and up the first steps leading to the second floor.

The money was in the bedroom against the far wall, tucked in a stocky safe behind a stack of shoeboxes in the closet. At least ten thousand. Any less and they wouldn't have risked it. While some may have chosen not to risk their lives for ten thousand dollars, for them, it placed the world in the palms of their hands—if only for the few weeks it lasted. Once it was gone, they'd have to roam the plains again, looking for prey to attack. But not tonight.

Tonight they would feast until they could eat no more.

They heard snoring once they reached the top of the stairs. Loud snoring. Like a chainsaw revving to life then choking off, only to rev to life once more. The dark figure paused to make sure the light-skinned figure behind heard the same thing. The snoring didn't originate down the hall, but from the first bedroom on the left. The door stood wide open. They peered inside and made out the sleeping figure of a large man. Light from the porno playing on a flat-screen TV cast a pale blue hue across his sleeping frame. His belly rose up and down like the torso of a beached whale gasping for air. Fat Freddy. He slept on a bare mattress with no sheet or blanket. The light figure pulled the door closed a little, but not all the way. They both nodded in understanding, then continued on.

The door to their destination was closed but unlocked. There was no furniture inside. Just a stack of boxes in the corner. Fat Freddy had just moved into the house from Macon, Georgia a month ago. Hadn't had time to unpack. He told them this the night before. They'd been there smoking and drinking. He didn't know anyone in Stone Mountain except his cousin. He didn't have to tell anyone that he sold dope. They'd been around enough hustlers to know what he did. He wasn't the man, but he was close to the man. Of that, they were sure. Close enough to keep a nice piece of change near him at all times. Could be *Go On the Run Money*, *Re-up Money*, or just *Trickin' Money*. Regardless, he had it, and they wanted it.

The safe sat in the closet exactly where it was supposed to be. The light-skinned goon moved the barrier of shoeboxes away in the darkness, while the dark-skinned figure posted up just outside the closet door, keeping one ear tuned to the bedroom down the hall where Fat Freddy's snores shook the walls.

The safe had been open the night before with the money laid stacked inside, looking like a green, shiny key that opened every door on the face of the Earth. They hadn't taken it then. That would have been foolish. If they had stolen it then, he would have known it was them and put out the word. People would have been looking for them. They decided to leave it and come back the next night. Tonight.

The light-skinned goon knelt beside the safe and tried the latch. Locked. The hand jiggled the latch a hundred times but the door would not open.

The dark-skinned figure squinted inside the closet, knowing something was wrong, and whispered, "What the fuck?"

"It's locked." The light-skinned figure stood quickly in the dark closet and brushed a shoebox overhead, causing it to tumble to the floor. The racket wasn't that loud, but it was loud enough.

They both paused. The dark-skinned goon gripped the taped handle of the twenty-two tightly. Fat Freddy wasn't snoring anymore. Time to go. They crept down the hall, both listening and hearing nothing but creaking sounds of the house and muffled cricket chirps outdoors. Even though their eyes had adjusted to the shadows, the hall seemed darker—more ominous than before. The dark-skinned goon led with the gun outstretched—waiting—hoping to hear Fat Freddy snoring again as they neared his bedroom to creep back down the stairs and out of the house.

"Who the fuck is in my crib?" Fat Freddy bumped into the gun as he stepped into the hallway.

The shot was more reaction than anything. Everything was dark, and then one bang of light floodlit the hallway, displaying the shock in Fat Freddy's eyes and the flower of red blooming from the new hole punched through his stained beater, right over his heart within a split second. Then darkness again. They heard the sound of Freddy hitting the wall behind him, then his fat ass wheezing on the floor.

The light-skinned figure felt along the wall for a light switch and flipped it on.

Fat Freddy lay in a pool of blood that spread wider with each passing second. His eyes were open as he stared up at the goons that shot him. A black Tech 9 handgun lay less than a foot from his limp right hand, but he looked too weak to reach for it. Freddy's eyes focused on the darker goon's green Grinch hat, thinking that it was a horrible sight to see right before he died.

The Grinch that stole his life.

"Help . . . me . . ." he wheezed.

The figures remained silent. Though both of them stared down on him, watching his life leak away with each pint of blood seeping on the carpeted floor. The dark one kept the trembling twenty-two trained on his face, even though he was no harm.

As Freddy lay there, he realized how vulnerable he was. He was willing to give them everything he had in exchange for one more day of life. He had a few thousand in his safe. A half-pound of heroin buried in the bathroom wall. He had three million stuffed into the mattress he slept on. They could have it all, as long as they called for an ambulance. He wouldn't tell the police a thing. What could he tell the cops? That someone shot him while robbing his house for drug money?

"Please . . ." he tried again. "I'll give you whatever you want. Just . . . help me . . ."

The goons exchanged a glance.

The light-skinned goon walked over to him and knelt by his side. "Tell me the combination to the safe and I'll call an ambulance."

He looked into the goon's green eyes and knew he had looked into them before, but it took too much energy to think of who it was. Each time his eyes blinked, they remained closed a little longer. The darkness invited him to delve deeper into its comforting depths. The pain dissipated when the darkness enveloped him. He felt nothing but the sweet sensation of slipping away from all the hurt he'd known in his life. He knew he was dying and he wanted to live, but he closed his eyes tighter begging for the release.

A hand slapped him. "Hey! You want to live? What's the combination?"

His mouth felt pasty. It was difficult to form words. His lips stuck. "Two . . . two . . ."

The hand slapped him again. His eyes opened. He must have passed out. *Let me sleep*, he wanted to say. The pain overwhelmed him when he was awake. He felt nothing when he slept. *Let me sleep*. He craved the peace of darkness, when coherence brought only pain and suffering.

The slap came once more. This time hard enough to make him wince.

"What's the goddamn combination? Two, two, what?"

His lungs would not expand. They felt flimsy, like a flat tire that wouldn't inflate. He tried to inhale, but failed.

"Two, two, what?"

Finally, euphoria rushed through his body. He stopped trying to breathe. Breath could do nothing for him anymore. He looked into the robber's eyes and knew exactly who it was. Anger was a foreigner in that moment. He felt only bliss as his soul left his body.

The word, "Seven . . ." slipped out with his last breath. He died with his eyes open.

The light-skinned figure stared down at him in amazement, having never seen a man die. The dark-skinned figure stood stock still with the gun still pointing down on Fat Freddy, afraid that his death was a trick and he'd awake to shoot them in the back if they let down their guard.

The combination was correct. It wasn't much money. Not as much as they hoped. Beside the money lay two chrome pistols. Both automatics. Maybe nine-millimeters. Brand new. The light-skinned goon stuffed the money and guns into a plastic department store bag they found in the closet, then hurried out of the room. It would have been smart to search the rest of the house, but the dark-skinned figure was still in the hallway, leaning against the wall, staring at Fat Freddy, traumatized.

"It's okay," the light-skinned figure said to the accomplice. "It was an accident." No way they could search the house now. They had to leave. They stepped over the body and the pool of blood surrounding it.

They didn't remove the masks until they were speeding away in the burgundy sedan that had been parked five houses down from Fat Freddy's.

TWO

MARCO PULLED UP TO THE AMACO on Peachtree at a quarter to three a.m. His black Mercedes 600 SL hummed into the empty spot beside a black Dodge Charger with charcoal black rims and windows tinted so dark that he could make out his clear reflection from two feet away. He saw his own face staring back at him, wearing a thin sleeve around his face and neck as a facemask.

The Charger's window rolled down. Jamal leaned back in the driver's seat with a caramel complexioned woman bouncing on his lap. Her top was down. She squeezed her own fat titties while panting and staring into Jamal's eyes as she rode him. She paid Marco no mind whatsoever as she worked for her pleasure. Jamal held up a lone index finger toward Marco. "Gimmie a minute." As the window rolled back up, Jamal told the girl, "You're gonna have to hurry this shit up." The Charger rocked harder for a few more minutes. Sounds of slapping bodies and the girl's screams came out muffled through the closed window.

Marco surveyed the gas station's parking lot so that he wouldn't pay attention to what was going on in Jamal's car. There was an attendant inside behind the cash register. A young black guy with short locks. The guy had his head angled down toward a phone in his hand. No one else was around because it was so late. Many people were holed up in their homes, swaddled in blankets to ward off the chill, fearful of catching Covid-19.

After ten minutes, the passenger door of the Charger opened and the woman climbed out wearing tight white leggings and a shimmering gold bubble coat. Surprisingly, her blonde hair cascaded down her shoulders and back perfectly, as if she hadn't been in Jamal's car working up a sweat. She glanced at Marco long enough for him to see that she wasn't black. She was some flavor of Latina—which he wasn't sure. But she was bad. Fat ass; plump lips; an ass that would make a horse jealous. She hurried to the driver's side of the Charger just as Jamal was climbing out. Jamal towered over the girl, standing at least six 'nine. He scooped her up in his arms and kissed her hard. She climbed into the driver's seat after he put her down. Then Jamal headed toward Marco's Mercedes. As an afterthought, Jamal knocked on the passenger-side window of his Charger. The window rolled down. He said, "Butterscotch, don't be having no niggas in my car."

"I won't, Daddy. Can't nobody do it like you do. Just hurry up and come back. I got something else for you." She flicked her tongue out at him, then Butterscotch pulled out of the parking spot and eased off into the night.

Jamal strutted to the passenger side of the Mercedes and opened the door. Before climbing in, Jamal pulled on a blue hospital face mask. Marco winced from the cold as a gust of frigid December air rushed in. It seeped right through his suede bomber jacket. He slunk his head down low inside the white fleece collar upturned against the back of his neck.

Jamal slammed the door. He looked to Marco with his lips twisted. "Fuck took you so long, Mondo? I been sitting here for almost an hour. I ain't got time to be waiting on niggas."

Marco shrugged. "Looked like you were doing just fine without me. Wish I had an hour like that. I thought about leaving and coming back. That's how much fun it looked like you were having."

Jamal smiled. "Funny guy."

"I had shit to do. Why didn't you meet me at the spot?"

"Genesis told me to have you drive your car. That's why."

Marco pulled out of the parking spot. "He's never done that before."

Jamal shook his head. "He probably wants us to put in some work. No sense in having two cars to keep up with. Better if we ride together. Less shit to keep up with."

Marco pulled out onto Peachtree. He hoped '*put in some work*' didn't mean what he thought it meant. Jamal had introduced Marco to Genesis less than a month ago. Since then he'd only been given menial tasks to do. All of the missions were relayed through Jamal. 'Pick up this money from here.' Or, 'Drop this bag off there.' Genesis was the biggest plug in Atlanta, but so far Marco had yet to see a crumb of dope in Genesis' hand. Anything Marco received came from Jamal. In the back of his mind, he knew Genesis was testing him. Trying to see if he could be trusted. No one trusted easily. Especially not in this life. Most dope dealers made it a rule to trust no one, but that rule came with an exception. A hustler had to trust somebody. Either his girl, wife, mama, or brother . . . he had to trust someone at some time. That was a fact of the drug game. No man could become a success on his own. He needed others to either run the show or take the fall.

"Turn here," Jamal said.

Marco did as he was told.

Jamal fingered the leather seat that he sat in. "Nice whip. I never seen you in this one. You usually push that raggedy Ford truck. What is it? An F250? How you afford some shit like this with what I'm pumping you?"

"Work."

"Yeah?" Jamal side-eyed him. "What kind of work you do?"

"I run a cellphone repair shop. It's over in Marietta. My man owns it. I manage it for him."

"Marietta? Over there with the crackers?" Jamal took a long look at Marco's clothes.

Marco was dressed in deblack crisp jeans, a button down shirt, and construction Timberlands. He wore a white gold bracelet and matching chain with a lion's head piece dangling over his belly. He kept his brush cut fresh and his short beard trimmed. His mahogany-colored skin was always clean and smooth.

Jamal asked, "There's a lot of money in fixing phones?"

"You wouldn't think so, but yeah. We replace an iPhone screen for three hundred. That's just the labor. Most places charge you four or five. Couple hundred a pop for profit."

Jamal nodded along. "You been copping work from me for three months now, and . . . make a right here . . . by this Zaxby's." Once Marco made the right turn, Jamal continued, "I been serving you for three months, and I never knew you had a job. Most niggas I know don't work. Hustling is their full-time job.'"

Marco shrugged. "That's where y'all fuck up. I pay my car and house notes with my work money. I play with the hustle money. Anything else I buy: furniture, clothes, jewelry; I pay cash for that shit. Everything major that I own is in my name. Feds can't fuck with me. I've got legitimate income. I pay my taxes."

Jamal nodded along. "Smart."

"Everything I do is smart."

Marco had met Jamal through Percy, a small-time hustler that Marco used to serve big eighths and halves to. Percy used to talk about Genesis all the time, explaining that he'd just been released from prison after serving a decade for trafficking, and now that Genesis was out, he had the streets on lock. Percy swore that he was going to stop copping from Marco and work for Genesis. But Percy had never met Genesis, only Jamal, who worked for Genesis. Eventually, Percy connected Marco and Jamal, and the rest was history. Marco started copping his weight from Jamal.

Jamal pointed. "Make this left."

Marco turned into a residential neighborhood. He passed luxury condos with BMWs and Corvettes parked in the driveways. "Is this where Genesis lives?"

Jamal ignored his question. "Pull up in front of that pink stucco joint right there. The one at the back of the cul-de-sac."

Marco pulled into the driveway behind a white Cadillac Escalade sitting beside a silver Benz G Wagon. He'd seen that Escalade before. It was Devon's. Genesis' right hand.

Marco and Jamal got out of the Mercedes and headed to the door. Jamal's fake swagger was legendary. He walked with a bop on the left leg that rolled his shoulders unevenly back and forth, like he hoisted the weight of the world with every step. It was the walk of a man who thought of himself as much more important than he really was.

The door opened before they had a chance to ring the bell. Devon stood in slacks and a white silk shirt that draped open three buttons down, broadcasting a Jesus piece dangling from a long platinum link. He was a pretty boy in his early forties with light skin and curly hair. He wore no facemask. "What the fuck took you so long?"

Jamal pushed past Devon while throwing a thumb over his shoulder toward Marco. "Ask Mr. Repairman back there. His fault. Not mine. I waited on that nigga for an hour."

Devon frowned toward Marco as he walked past. Marco said, "I had to close down my job. Took a minute."

Devon nodded in understanding. "Don't worry about it."

Genesis shot pool on a black table upholstered with gold felt in a spacious living room. The balls were clear glass stained in a rainbow of colors. He wore black Jordan's, black jeans, and a black hoodie. No jewelry. No watch. Genesis was a dark man in his early fifties with a slick bald head. He wasn't short. He wasn't tall. He was that perfect height that placed him between giants and midgets with an equality that demanded respect from both. He stared at Jamal as he strode into the room and plopped down on a soft leather couch.

Marco stood just in the doorway, waiting to be admitted into the room.

Jamal asked Genesis, "Where's your mask?"

"What the fuck do I need a mask for when you're wearing one?"

Jamal shrugged. "I was just asking."

Genesis leaned on his pool cue as he stared at Jamal. "You think you run shit because you're my cousin, don't you?"

Jamal reeled back, offended. "What I say?"

"Whatever the fuck you want to say. That's the problem." Genesis laid his pool cue on the table and pointed to Marco. "Come out back. I want to talk to you."

Marco followed Genesis to a sliding glass door at the back of the house. Genesis grabbed a black leather jacket and slung it around his shoulders as he stepped out. Marco spotted the butt of a chrome automatic sticking out of Genesis' waistband at the small of his back just before the jacket settled comfortably on his body. He followed Genesis into the cold night.

Once outside, Genesis pulled out a pack of Newport's and lit one. He held out the pack to Marco.

Marco shook his head. "Don't smoke."

Genesis nodded. Up close, Marco could see every bit of Genesis' age. Even though Genesis was a drug dealer, he had businessman qualities that lifted him higher up in the food chain. Genesis made up for the education he missed in school while serving time in prison. He spoke like a man who had read many books, and Marco knew that he couldn't fool a thoughtful man like that. Genesis was too intelligent and too cunning, so he never tried to fool him. He learned to play his position as a silent subordinate willing to obey at all costs. He'd learned long ago that in some situations loyalty would take him further than ambition.

"I like you, Mondo," Genesis began. "I don't meet people. No need in this life. But I wanted to meet you."

"Why is that?"

"I heard good things about you." Genesis took a hit on his cigarette. "And . . . because I need someone I can trust."

Marco looked through the window and saw Devon enter the living room with a beer in his hand. "What about Devon?"

"I trust Devon, but you've got to use people for what they're good at. He's a hustler. Not a leader. You don't place a cook in a cashier's position. Different skillset."

Marco waited for more. When no more came, he asked, "Jamal?"

Genesis flicked his half-smoked cigarette over the railing of the back deck into the darkness. "There is no more Jamal."

Marco held his gaze, feeling that the comment was directed toward him somehow. Jamal sat on the sofa playing a video game with an unlit blunt hanging from his mouth. How could there be no Jamal when he was sitting right there on the couch? "What'd he do?"

Genesis looked into the living room. Marco followed his gaze. Genesis said, "This is a thinking man's game, Mondo. Children get killed because they do childish things. They trust the wrong people. Misguided trust has consequences."

Marco's heart sank as he wondered how much Genesis knew. He thought of the steel idling in Genesis' waistband while at the same time he thought of the forty-five hunkered in his own, and hoped he wouldn't have to use it.

Genesis turned back to Marco. "Percy was a rat, Mondo. He got knocked with a quarter Ki of white a month ago. They found it in his fucking hand, and he never spent a night in jail. The Feds are going to raid Jamal's crib tomorrow night, but he doesn't know it."

"Percy was a rat? What happened to him?"

"I don't know what happened to Percy, but he's not a rat anymore. I promise you that. He won't have the chance to tell anything else. That's why they need Jamal. They'll pressure him until he talks. He ain't never been locked up. He can't hold his mud. He's my cousin, but he's weak. Too weak to go to war with the wolves. You know what I mean? Young niggas get into this game thinking they'll live like DMX in *Belly*. They don't realize the work they have to put in. It's easy to hustle and make money. It's hard to maintain that shit when you've got niggas and cops threatening to kick in your door every five minutes. Dealing with that shit is the hard part."

Marco turned toward Jamal again. He was engaged in the game, oblivious to what was now obvious to Marco. "When do you want it done?"

Genesis stared at Marco for a long time, looking pleased at his intuition. "Tonight. You and Devon will take him somewhere. I don't want to know where. I don't want to know how. I don't want to know anything. Just take him as far away from here as possible. I don't want to see him again."

Marco nodded once. "Okay."

Devon was already zipped in his leather coat when they made it back into the house. He stood by the front door.

Marco walked up to Jamal and said, "We gotta go. Genesis . . ."

"Lead the way." Jamal threw the video game controller on the coffee table in front of him.

Genesis stepped to Jamal as they headed toward the door. Jamal held out his hand for a shake. Genesis took the hand and pulled Jamal into a tight embrace that he held for a moment. As a show of love, Genesis kissed Jamal on the cheek. For Jamal it may have been a gesture of endearment, but Marco knew it was the kiss of death. When he let Jamal go, they stepped out into the cold night. Genesis closed the door softly behind them.

Forty minutes later, they pulled over near a secluded wooded area, miles from any sign of civilization. Devon sat in the backseat. Jamal sat in the passenger's. Jamal had been texting for the whole ride, and only paused when the car stopped moving.

Jamal put his phone away. "Where are we?"

"Somewhere in Kennesaw," Marco lied.

Jamal looked around the silent road. "We waiting on somebody?"

Devon said, "We're going to them. You bring a burner?"

Jamal shook his head. "Nah."

Devon chuckled. "Un-fucking-be-lieveable. Just like you to rely on me for everything."

"I was with my girl when Genesis called. I had my hand on her ass, not my gun. How was I supposed to know what Genesis wanted? What the fuck?"

Devon reached over the seat and dangled a twenty-five in Jamal's face. "Take my back up. You're gonna need it."

They got out of the car and began walking down the street. It was dark out. Marco saw no homes or lights as they walked.

"Where are we going?" Jamal asked.

Both Devon and Marco held back as Jamal walked on. "Keep walking," Devon told Jamal. Then Devon nudged Marco and whispered, "Hit him from the back. Hurry up." Devon gestured for Marco to get it over with.

Marco pulled out his forty-five and quietly racked the slide. Devon stopped walking all together. Marco pointed the gun as he followed Jamal, aiming at his head.

Suddenly Jamal stopped walking. He spun around with the twenty-five pointed at Marco's face. "Fuck you pointing that gun at me, Mondo?"

Marco never stopped walking.

"Mondo?" Jamal said again, then pulled the trigger. The gun dry-fired. He pulled it again and again. Nothing happened. He looked at the gun in his hand, then to Devon staring at him. "You motherfucker. What are you trying to pull, Devon? Does Genesis know about this? I knew your shiesty ass was trying to get between us. Jealous bitch. What did you tell him?"

"Do it, Mondo," Devon said. "We need to get back."

Marco heard him, but instead of pulling the trigger, he whispered, "Run," to Jamal.

Jamal screwed up his face. "What?"

Marco walked a little closer and tried to keep his voice low enough so Devon would not hear. "Run. Go. You want to live?" When Jamal ran, he would shoot wide, missing him by a mile.

"Run?" Jamal asked. "So you can shoot me in the back?"

Devon hurried closer with his gun level with Jamal's head. "Mondo, you told Genesis you could do this. Get it done. Don't make me have to pop this nigga for you. Genesis won't like that. He might make me pop you next."

Devon stepped too close. Jamal dipped left, then right as he bolted toward Devon. He slapped Marco's gun hand away and yanked Devon's gun right out of his grip while punching him in the face. Devon reeled back and shielded his eyes when Jamal lifted the weapon to shoot.

Marco spun with his pistol ready. "Jamal!" He screamed as he fired. Two forty-five slugs ripped through Jamal's ribcage and punched twin holes in his heart before exploding out the other side. Marco stood horrified as Jamal's lifeless body dropped to the asphalt.

Devon ran over and pried his gun out of Jamal's hand. He wiped a trickle of blood from the corner of his mouth and aimed down on Jamal's still body. He pulled the trigger, lighting up the night with six shots that tore into Jamal's chest. Marco winced with each shot.

"I bet you won't hit me no more," Devon declared after unloading. Then he turned to Marco. "I won't tell Genesis what happened if you don't." He wiped a trickle of blood from his nose, then he kicked Jamal's lifeless body. "Welcome to the organization." Devon started back toward Marco's Mercedes.

Marco stared down at Jamal's body lying twisted on the ground, and he wondered if the price of loyalty was worth the risk of losing his soul.

THREE

H E PUSHED ROCHELLE AGAINST THE WALL and pinned her there so that she couldn't move. His lips pressed hard against hers. She wanted to mutter "no," but he kissed her so passionately that she couldn't form the words with her mouth. Her hands rose to his chest and shoved gently. Her effort proceeded without conviction and subsided once his hands dropped to the soft curve of her plump ass. He gripped a cheek in his palm, and Rochelle lost her mind. He pulled his body against hers. She felt his hard dick straining in his pants against her leg.

She wore only a red, silk robe and a pair of red, lace panties. He pulled the robe open forcefully and clawed at her heavy breasts beneath. Her head swooned in delight as he tugged her nipples. Rochelle's mouth yawned open in pleasure. Her pussy flooded her panties, and she wanted to take them off. His hands roamed her body as if she didn't have the right to protest. She had never been treated so forcefully. The helpless way that she felt turned her on even more. Rochelle needed to be possessed. She needed to be taken roughly. She needed to feel the long, hard length of him pounding in and out of her sopping wet pussy. She needed to feel his hands gripping her hips so tightly that she couldn't get away as he fucked her as hard as he could.

His hand crept between her legs to rub her pussy through her panties. She thrust her sex out to him, inviting him to probe deeper. Seconds later, she felt his fingers slip beneath her panties. Rochelle lost her breath when one slid inside of her. She reached down and gripped his dick, loving the warm heat of his skin against hers. She wanted that hard dick inside of her. She jacked him slowly as he fingered her. Rochelle spread her legs a bit and rolled the tip of his dick against the mouth of her vagina, determined to put it in and let him fuck her chest to chest as they stood there.

"Rochelle!"

She heard the voice calling her name, yet she focused on the fingers probing her moist middle. She moved his fingers aside and jammed his dick into her slowly. The voice was an annoyance that she didn't care to acknowledge.

"Rochelle! Wake up!"

The man stepped back, leaving Rochelle panting against the wall. She reached out to snatch him back to her, but her hand slipped through his body like it would have slipped through a ghost's ethereal form. He faded further and further away until he disappeared into darkness, as if he had never existed in the first place.

Rochelle opened her eyes and stared up at the white ceiling. Her comforter was twisted around her body and between her legs, but she didn't need a blanket to ward off the chill. She was on fire. Her own hand was wedged between her legs. She was so wet that she wondered if she'd been playing with herself in her sleep.

"Rochelle," Cotton said. "It's seven-fifteen. You're gonna be late for work. Get your ass up."

Rochelle looked toward the doorway and spotted her high-yellow roommate, Cotton, standing there in just a black thong and sheer black robe. Cotton leaned against the doorframe like a model posing for the cameras. Her white, blonde afro ballooned out in a soft halo.

"I'm up," Rochelle told her.

Cotton smiled. "You better be." She bit a corner of her bottom lip. "Thought I was gonna have to come in there and rough you up."

"Nah," Rochelle quipped. "You might like it too much."

"Whatever. *You* might like it too much."

Cotton turned to leave. Rochelle noticed how short Cotton's robe was as she walked away. It stopped just at the small of her back, leaving the expanse of her fat yellow ass exposed as she switched down the hall. Rochelle found it hard to look away. She didn't have an ass as fat or as round and perfect as Cotton's. Not many women did. Yet it wasn't jealousy that kept her eyes glued to her roommate's backside.

Rochelle rolled over onto her side. She closed her eyes and tried to recall an image of the man in her dream, but he was a mystery. His face was so blank that she wondered if she'd seen a face at all. Memories of Cotton standing in her doorway took over her thoughts. Her fingers dipped between her legs. She was still soaking wet. It had been so long since she'd fucked a man. Almost a year. She rolled out of bed knowing that she'd have to get laid soon, or she would go crazy.

Rochelle walked to her dresser and opened the top drawer. Beneath a stack of folded panties were six bundles of banded bills resting beside a loaded Berretta nine-millimeter. She pulled one wad out and yanked off the rubber band. She counted four-thousand dollars. It wasn't a lot, but it was four-thousand more than what she had before. She and Cotton had made a good lick the night before, but she would need more than four-thousand a night to accomplish her goal. Rochelle wrapped the money up, dropped it back into the drawer and headed to the shower.

Cotton was in the kitchen scrambling eggs when Rochelle entered after brushing her teeth and showering. Rochelle wore a blue terry cloth robe and slippers, nothing beneath. Cotton stood before the stove in just her robe and panties. Her plump breasts hung free beneath the see-through robe. Rochelle walked to the refrigerator and pulled out a bottle of orange juice that was almost empty. She popped the cap and turned the bottle up. Once she finished the bottle, she leaned against the counter and stared at her roommate.

Cotton stood at five 'three. She was so high-yellow that most people thought she was white from a distance. She wore emerald eyes so green that a fifty-dollar bill would get jealous at the sight of them. Her face was light and peppered with tan freckles, but you had to really pay attention to notice. Her flat belly tapered into wide hips and an ass so pretty that many women went broke trying to duplicate what she had been born with.

Rochelle was a little taller, a little slimmer, and brown-skinned. There was nothing extraordinary about her appearance. She wore her hair in a puffball at the top of her head. She cleaned up nice, but rarely had a reason to dress to impress.

Cotton asked, "You want some of these eggs?"

Rochelle brought her eyes up to Cotton's. "I'll get something at work."

Cotton sucked her teeth while shoveling eggs onto a nearby plate. "Alright now. Living off of donuts and coffee will blow you up. Your ass is already getting fatter."

"It is not."

Cotton put down the skillet and turned off the stove. "Shit." She walked over to Rochelle and lifted the back of her robe exposing her brown behind. Cotton sucked her teeth again. "That thing is getting round." She reached down and ran a slow hand over one of Rochelle's plump ass cheeks.

"Cotton. Stop."

Cotton looked into Rochelle's eyes. "Why?" She cupped Rochelle's ass cheek and squeezed. "Maybe you should keep eating donuts. You are what you eat. They're making your ass softer."

Rochelle reached down and pulled her hand away. "Cotton, I'm not trying to get anything started with you."

Cotton walked up on Rochelle and stood breast to breast. Their lips poised less than an inch apart, so close that Rochelle could feel Cotton's breath beating against her lips when she said, "Just let me taste it. You don't have to lick me back." Cotton kissed Rochelle on the neck. Her hand dipped beneath the folds of the robe and touched Rochelle's naked pussy. "See how wet you are? Let me lick it. Come on. Please." Her fingers tickled Rochelle's stiff clit, making her hips roll in a circle. A finger slipped into Rochelle's pussy and massaged her front wall as it curled in a come here motion, then it slid out and rolled over her clit again.

Rochelle leaned into the kiss. Cotton's fingers rubbing her pussy made her feel warm all over. Any more of that fondling, and she would cum on her hand. But Rochelle eased along the kitchen counter and slid away. "Cotton . . ."

Cotton stood there, staring at Rochelle with a devious smile staining her face. "You let me please you before. Why not now?"

Rochelle wrapped her robe tighter around her body and retreated to a far wall. "It was one time, Cotton. I'm not . . . I'm not *that* way."

Cotton stared deeply into her eyes. "Did it feel good to you?"

Rochelle nodded. "You know it did. But . . . I'm not trying to go there again. I love you, Cotton . . . as a sister . . . nothing else."

Cotton shrugged and walked back to her eggs. "You'll want me when you realize a man ain't good for nothing but fucking for an hour. They ain't worth a damn for the other twenty-three. A woman knows what you need."

Just then, Lacy hurried into the kitchen wearing an oversized Tweety Bird nightshirt and a scarf around her permed hair. Her white friend, Bunny, followed with her long red hair feathering behind her. Rochelle noted that Bunny was dressed in gray leggings and a black bubble coat. Her boots were laced tight. She hadn't spent the night, for once. Bunny had probably climbed in through Lacy's bedroom window.

"Morning," Lacy said to the room.

Cotton barely looked over her shoulder to say, "Hey."

Rochelle assumed Cotton was still fuming from her rejection. Rochelle turned to Lacy. "You looking for a job today? College tuition isn't free. I'm busting my ass to help you out, but I could use some assistance."

Lacy eyed Cotton's eggs and pulled the carton out of the refrigerator. She plucked a bowl from the dishwasher and cracked four eggs into it. Bunny pulled out butter and a loaf of bread. Lacy told Rochelle, "I don't have to go to college."

"You do," Rochelle assured her. "You already took a year off after graduating high school. You wasted that time ripping and running the streets with this one . . ." she pointed to Bunny. "You'll be nineteen in two weeks. You had your fun. You met your boys. Now it's time to prepare for your future."

Lacy used the same skillet Cotton had used to cook her eggs. She dropped a pat of butter inside and let it sizzle to liquid. "I'm going to get a job. One day."

"Not one worth a damn, Lacy. Do you want to work two jobs like me? I'm twenty-five with nothing to show for it. Cotton is twenty-eight, and she dances for a living."

Cotton paused chewing to say, "I make damn good money too. And I don't punch no clock."

Lacy smiled. "Did you hear that? Maybe I'll dance at the club with Cotton."

Rochelle rolled her eyes. "I'm not saying anything is wrong with that. Y'all gonna fuck around and catch covid. But Lacy, there is a better life out there for you. Don't get stuck living in the hood because that's all you see. Don't sell yourself short."

Rochelle watched Lacy pour the scrambled eggs into the skillet and stir them. Bunny hopped up on the counter beside the stove, a spot she'd been sitting on since she was twelve years old. Rochelle looked at her little sister with sad eyes. The girl was hardheaded. She couldn't see that only death and hardship was the result of living a purposeless life. Skinny and brown-skinned, Lacy still acted like the teenaged girl her body was built like.

Rochelle looked to Bunny. For a white girl, Bunny was built like a sister. Wide hips and a fat ass spread on the countertop. She had big titties and a cute little face. She wasn't very tall, but she was tough. Bunny had grown up in Decatur with black people her whole life. Rochelle didn't think Bunny could pretend to act white if she had to. She knew that Bunny was part of Lacy's problem. Bunny's mother was a heroin addict who used her beauty to trap men into taking care of her and had no ambition to do anything for herself. Like her mother, Bunny seemed to have no ambition. She was content with getting her belly full at the end of the night, and most of the time, she was eating Rochelle's food, because there was none to eat in her own house. As long as Lacy hung out with Bunny, she would not see school as her way out of the 'hood'.

Lacy told Bunny, "Grab two plates from the cabinet."

Bunny slid off the counter and grabbed two plates. She sat them down and loaded the toaster with two pieces of bread.

Lacy glanced to Rochelle as she scooped sizzling eggs onto the plates. "Mama didn't go to college. She did okay."

Rochelle shook her head. "She did. Ended up with a bullet in her head because her drug dealing boyfriend couldn't pay his debts."

Lacy turned to Rochelle with hurt in her eyes. "But we were doing okay when she was alive. Michael might have been selling drugs, but we were living good."

"How the hell would you know what living good is? You were twelve years old when Mama was murdered. You had some toys. That is not what living good is. But if you don't go to school, you're going to find out what living hard is like, and real fucking soon. I won't have you living under my roof if you aren't working or going to school. You have to do something.

I'm not going to keep taking care of a grown-ass woman who doesn't know how to take care of herself."

The toast popped up. Bunny slid a piece onto Lacy's plate and one onto her own, then she started eating.

Lacy said, "I'll look for a job today, but I'll need to borrow your car."

Rochelle shook her head. "Hell no. You left me on fumes last time. I barely made it to the gas station to fill up."

"Rochelle," Lacy complained, "I'll fill it up this time."

"With what money? Neither you, or that pale heifer you call a friend, have two nickels to rub together between the two of you."

Lacy recoiled, looking offended. "I have money. Soon I'll have enough to buy my own car." Bunny cleared her throat, drawing Lacy's attention. Lacy stopped talking.

Rochelle snickered. "Where'd you get money? You must have stolen it from somebody because you damn sure didn't earn it."

Lacy looked to Bunny before saying, "Santa Claus gave it to me."

Cotton snorted a laugh, then walked out of the kitchen.

Rochelle cocked her head to the side. "Tell Santa to give you a car for Christmas, because you won't be borrowing mine. And while you're at it, ask Santa to give you a life."

FOUR

MARCO PULLED INTO THE STRIP MALL at a quarter to eight in the morning and parked next to a plain burgundy sedan. The gunmetal gray sky loomed above like doom ready to rain down its fury on the Earth. It was murderously cold out, and he regretted having to step out in it. He pulled his bomber jacket tighter and slipped on a short, tan beanie before getting out of his Benz.

Colorful Confections Donut and Cupcake Shop stood out from the Aldi's beside it. The bright red sign boasting Christmas Delights drew his attention as he headed past it toward the cell phone store. He looked inside the donut shop for a second, and the woman he saw behind the register made him pause in his tracks.

She was brown-skinned with a black facemask over her beautiful face. He couldn't see her entire face, behind the mask, but he was drawn to her all the same. The red apron she wore over a white T-shirt did nothing to hide the curves beneath. She wore a green Grinch hat with a fuzzy white ball on top. She looked up and locked eyes with Marco as he stood on the sidewalk outside the store. He swore that he saw a smile, but he couldn't be sure. Her eyes narrowed, but the shape of her lips was a mystery behind the facemask. If she had smiled at all, it disappeared faster than it had appeared on her face. She looked away.

Marco glanced toward the cell phone repair shop. He needed to get a job there to keep up the lie he'd told Jamal. He had called ahead and spoken to the owner, but he needed to see the man face to face. He looked at the cell phone repair shop. It would be open all day. It could wait.

He pulled a white facemask over his mouth and lips, then he walked into the donut shop.

The woman was already helping a middle-aged white guy when Marco stepped to the counter. She looked his way, then continued placing red velvet cupcakes into a cupcake holder. She and the guy were having a friendly conversation. She asked about his wife and his son, so Marco assumed he came in there on the regular. Marco moved down the counter, looking at the cupcakes and donuts on display on the wall behind her.

The woman put the cupcakes in a bag and said, "Have a nice day," to her customer as he headed to the front door. She glanced at Marco and walked down the counter toward him. "And what can I help you with today?"

Marco tried his best to suppress a smile. Then he remembered that he was wearing a mask, and she couldn't see if he was smiling or not. He looked into her almond shaped eyes and couldn't think of a thing to say.

"Sir?"

He rubbed his eyes. *Don't make a fool of yourself.* "I was walking past the window, and I was wondering . . . what's your name?"

She cocked her head to the side. "You didn't come in here to buy something?"

He shook his head slowly, wanting her to know that he had only entered the store to talk to her.

Instead of giving in to his flattery, she turned and walked in the other direction. She grabbed a wet towel from a sink below the counter and began wiping down the counter top.

"Hey," Marco said. "I just want to talk to you."

She kept wiping the counter and did not look up. "I'm working. I don't have time to talk."

"Are you serious?" Marco walked down to where she was. "I think you're gorgeous. At least let me put a name to the face."

She punched a hand to her hip. "You think you're the first man that has come in here wanting to know my name? My phone number? Where I live? Or my bra size? Get in line."

"I didn't ask for all that."

"You asked for enough. And if you're not going to make a purchase, I'm going to have to ask you to leave."

"Damn. All I want to know is your name."

"I don't want to give it to you."

Just then, a balding dark-skinned man walked out from the back carrying a load of fresh cupcakes. His white facemask was stained yellow with sweat. He looked to the woman, "Rochelle, would you open that display cabinet there?"

Marco smiled. "Rochelle . . ."

Rochelle sighed and looked to her co-worker. "Bobby!"

Bobby stopped with his eyebrows raised. "What? I do something wrong?"

"No." She opened the display case and watched as he placed a couple dozen Rudolph the Red-nosed Reindeer themed cupcakes into it. She glanced at Marco casually and rolled her eyes each time their gazes met. When Bobby was finished loading the cabinet, she asked him, "Do you need help in the back?"

"Nope." He looked to Marco standing in the lobby. "Looks like you've got a customer anyway."

Marco chuckled.

Bobby winked at him.

Rochelle huffed.

When Bobby made his way into the back, Marco leaned on the counter. "Rochelle. That's a nice name. Pretty. Almost as pretty as you."

"You don't know what I look like. I'm wearing a mask. I don't know what you look like either."

Marco stepped back from the counter and pulled one ear strap of his mask free, revealing his handsome face. "I'm not so bad, am I?"

She rolled her eyes. "Good looks does not determine a good man."

Marco pulled his mask back on. "You won't let me win, will you?"

She stood in front of him. "You know my name now. You gonna ask me on a date? Promise to take me someplace nice? Try to get me to a hotel room?"

Marco shook his head. "Nah."

"What are you going to say? I've heard it all before. Go ahead ask me."

Marco smiled. "You got any donuts with Santa faces on them?"

Rochelle smirked. "Really?"

"You said I needed to leave if I didn't buy something. I'll buy one of those."

Rochelle searched his eyes. "We don't have donuts like that. Just red or green or sprinkled. We have cookies with Santa and cupcakes with Santa. No donuts. Guess you'll have to leave empty handed. Sorry."

"I'll take a dozen Santa cupcakes."

Rochelle paused before moving to fill the order. "Just a dozen?"

Marco shrugged. "Two. Three. I'll buy you out if it'll make you smile. I don't give a damn about the cupcakes. I didn't come in here for cupcakes. I came in here because I thought you were fine as hell through that window, but if I have to buy a cupcake or two to get your attention, then I might as well buy a thousand to keep it. I'll spend all of my money just to get one glimpse of your face."

Rochelle stared at him. Then she picked up a napkin, turned, and walked to the display case. She plucked out one Santa themed cupcake and brought it back. She leaned over the counter and held it out to him. "This one is on the house. You can't buy my attention. You have to earn it."

Marco took the cupcake slowly and bit into it while staring into her eyes. It was sweet and soft and delicious. Exactly how he imagined Rochelle would taste if he ever had the opportunity to sample her pleasures.

She watched him eat for a moment, then she asked, "Are you a cop?"

He stopped chewing. "Why do you ask that?"

"You came in here asking for donuts."

He laughed. "Just because I like donuts doesn't mean I'm a cop. I'm not above any job though, if you're asking. I'll do whatever it takes to get the money, and as much as I can in as short a time as possible. If being a cop does that, give me an application."

"I don't like cops. I like hustlers."

Marco took another bite of his cupcake and finished it before saying, "We're all hustlers. Even the trash man is a hustler when he sees something of value. It's in our nature to hustle—to get ahead in any way we can. Anybody who doesn't is a sucker."

Rochelle regarded him with curious eyes. Marco found himself feeling self-conscious under her gaze. He wondered if he had a piece of cake on his lip. Did he smell okay? Was his beanie crooked? She didn't stare at him as if something was wrong, rather, she stared at him as a fighter would size up an opponent. She measured him with her eyes as if she were deciding if he meant what he said about hustling and money.

Rochelle unhooked one strap of her facemask and allowed him to see her face.

Breath caught in Marco's throat at the sight of her. She was even more beautiful than he had imagined.

She put her mask back on. "I'm still not going out with you," she said.

"I haven't asked."

"Not yet."

Marco laughed. "Who said I was going to ask?"

"You will."

"I don't have your phone number."

"I'm not giving you that. I don't trust easily."

Marco stared at her in amazement. "What makes you think I'm going to ask you out?"

She said, "You're going to write your phone number on a napkin and drop it on the counter when you leave. You'll ask me out when—and if—I call you."

"If . . . you call me?"

She nodded. "We've been talking for a few minutes, so I know you're not deaf. I said *if* I call you."

"Got a pen?"

Rochelle reached beneath the counter and pulled up a napkin and a ball point pen. She laid them in front of him and watched carefully as Marco wrote down his name and number. He spun the napkin around when he finished. She picked it up and stuffed it into her pocket.

"That's it?" he asked.

"You've gotten a lot farther than the other men who waltz up in here telling me that I must have fallen from heaven."

He chuckled. "I'll leave before you change your mind."

Rochelle shrugged. "I don't change my mind."

Marco turned and headed toward the front door.

When he put his hand on the handle, Rochelle called out, "Marco."

He turned, remembering how fast she read his name on the napkin. "I saw you through the window. I thought you were cute too. You earned my attention."

"Call me." Marco stepped out into the frigid winter air feeling warm inside.

FIVE

L ACY TURNED TO BUNNY. "It's cold as fuck out here. We need to hurry up and buy a car."

The sun had just gone down, leaving the sky above stained dark purple. They were walking in Decatur toward a Citgo gas station. Both were huddled in thick coats to fight off the chill. Bunny had her long hair tucked under a gray toboggan, and Lacy's head was covered with her signature Grinch hat. They both wore their facemasks.

"Yeah," Lacy agreed. "One with some heat."

A gold Chrysler 300, sitting on twenty-inch chrome BBS rims, sat double parked at an angle in front of the store. A young man sat in the passenger seat rolling a blunt as Lacy and Bunny neared the car. Lacy stared inside as she walked past, meeting the young man's eyes. He did not wear a facemask.

The guy hopped out of the car as soon as he got a good look at her. "A yo, shorty!"

Lacy exchanged a glance with Bunny, but neither turned back to him.

"You . . ." he said. "The Grinch that stole my heart. Slow down."

The girls kept walking. He hurried in front of them with the half-rolled blunt still in his hand. He was dark-skinned with a wavy brush cut. Dimples creased his cheeks when he smiled. He wore Jordan One's, skinny black jeans, and a black leather jacket. His long chain swayed against his chest with the weight of a heavy Jesus piece. Diamond earrings sparkled from each ear in the gas station lamp light.

Lacy looked into his eyes and knew that she would fuck him. She would fuck the hell out of him.

He asked, "Did y'all hear me calling?"

Lacy shrugged. His accent sounded like he came from up north. Maybe New Jersey. "Social distance, Mr. I ain't wearing a mask. My name ain't shorty."

"What is it?"

Lacy pursed her lips and tried to walk around him.

He stepped in front of her again. "Hold up, ma. What's your name?"

"I don't talk to strangers who don't wear masks."

He smiled at that. "How do you get to be friends with someone if you never talk to them?"

Lacy crossed her arms. "Who said I was looking for a friend?"

His smile faded. "That's how you're gonna act? Fuck you then." He turned to walk away.

Bunny nudged Lacy in the ribs. "Wait," Lacy said. "I thought you wanted to know my name."

"I ain't got time to waste on no bitch that thinks she's better than me. I don't play games. I get money. If you don't want to give me your name . . . I don't give a fuck. There are plenty of bitches out here that do." He headed back to the car.

Lacy cleared her throat. "My name is Lacy."

He stared at her. "They call me Dame."

Lacy gestured to Bunny. "This is my girl Bunny. She doesn't talk much."

Dame looked her over. "Does she fuck?"

Lacy looked to Bunny, then back to Dame. "Yeah. She fucks. Depending on who it is."

Dame's smile widened. "Good. My cousin Rich loves white girls." He opened the back door to the Chrysler. "Y'all want a ride?"

They were cruising in the Chrysler twenty-minutes later with Dame's cousin Rich at the wheel. Dame sat in the passenger seat and passed his lit blunt around. Lacy thought the weed was pretty good. He called it Bluebird Kush, but to her it was just a step up from some Reggie that she could have bought anywhere. It did the trick though. Soon after getting in the car, she was high and listening to Rick Ross booming on the stereo. She and Bunny exchanged looks and smiles, knowing the night was going to be a wild one. They had taken off their masks. Thoughts of catching the corona didn't bother them as much as it should have. They were more concerned with having a good time.

Rich looked a lot older than Dame. Dame told Lacy that he was twenty-three, but she suspected he was younger than that. Maybe around her and Bunny's age. Nineteen. Rich must have been in his thirties. It was obvious who called the shots. Rich let Dame do all the talking, and talking was what Dame did best, but when Rich threw Dame a stern look, Dame quieted down. Dame explained that he had recently moved from New York to get money in Atlanta with Rich. Rich was from Atlanta. Dame was a rapper and had a show coming up at a club in College Park. He invited Lacy and Bunny, promising to get them in for free and pay for their drinks. Rich remained quiet the whole ride. Lacy noticed him glance at Bunny occasionally through the rearview mirror, but he said nothing. Lacy thought the two would be a perfect match. Both quiet.

Lacy told Dame very little about herself. What was the point? She would never date him. She might give him the pussy, but that was just to make sure she wasn't bored. There was no need for them to get to know each other. If he played his cards right, she'd give him some head before he hit it. He didn't need to know her Social Security number for that.

They pulled up to a nice townhouse in Stone Mountain. It was a modest place, but nice.

A big, black Rottweiler greeted them at the door when they entered. The dog jumped on Bunny as soon as she stepped in. "Down, Saint!" Rich yelled while grabbing the dog.

Bunny moved Rich's hand away from the pooch. "It's okay," she said, looking into his eyes. "I like dogs."

Rich nodded and backed away. "He only likes pretty girls."

Bunny smiled. "You must bring a lot over here."

Rich smirked. "Enough. None as pretty as you though."

Bunny didn't say anything after that. She petted the dog's head for a moment, then pushed him away. When the dog was clear, she stepped close to Rich and laid a hand on his coat above his heart. "Do you have a bedroom?"

Rich nodded. "Come on." He took her by the hand and led her up the stairs to a dark corridor.

Lacy and Dame stood at the bottom of the stairs, watching.

Dame looked to Lacy. "She don't waste no time, huh?"

Lacy shrugged. "I told you she fucks."

Dame licked his lips in anticipation. "Do you?"

Lacy bit her bottom lip. "Not right now. In a little while. Let me see your house."

"Ain't much to see." Dame took her by the hand and walked her into the cluttered living room. "Shit ain't clean. We've been chilling in the house to stop from catching that Covid shit." As they walked, Dame got a text. He read it, then he fired one off. A second later he responded to another.

Lacy looked at him. "You need to make a phone call or something?"

He shook his head. "Nah. My man wants to see me, but we've got time to kick it. If he shows up, it'll only be for a few minutes. Come on."

The place was furnished like any bachelor's pad would be. Mismatched couches, a dinged up coffee table, a halogen lamp in the corner. The seventy-inch television was the nicest thing in the place, and that was because it was hooked up to a PlayStation with the controllers strewn about the floor as if Dame and Rich hadn't expected company or didn't care who came over.

The kitchen was surprisingly clean. "Want a drink?" Dame asked her.

"Got any Vodka?"

He nodded. "Absolut. Orange juice?"

"Just Vodka. No ice."

He pulled out a bottle from the freezer and poured her a shot in a regular glass. She threw it back and swallowed it in one gulp.

When she put the glass down, she asked Dame, "Do you think I'm pretty?"

"Hell yeah."

Lacy looked around the kitchen. Out the window, she noticed the neighbor's lights on. She wondered who lived there. "Is it hot in here?" She unzipped her coat and pulled it off, revealing the tight white shirt beneath. Dame's eyes dropped to her breasts. They weren't Double-E's like Bunny's, but they were round and nice. She stepped close to Dame. Close enough to rub her breasts against his chest. "I don't want a boyfriend. I don't want a man. I just want to fuck. Can you do that? Can you fuck me good and then take me home in the morning?"

Dame searched her eyes. "Uh . . . yeah. Hell yeah."

She pulled open his leather jacket and planted kisses against his neck. Her fingers found his crotch and tried to unbutton his pants.

"Wait," he said. He reached down and pulled a chrome automatic from his waistband. He placed it on the counter.

Lacy looked at the gun and pretended that its presence didn't bother her. She stuffed her hand inside his pants and found him hot and hard for her. "You've got a big dick." She pulled it out, stroked it in her hand and whispered, "You want me to suck it?"

Dame nodded. "Hell yeah."

Lacy giggled. "Is that all you know how to say? Hell yeah?"

"Hell yeah."

Lacy dropped to her knees before him. She lied. His dick wasn't big. It was average. It was a little skinny for her taste. Yet she took him in her mouth and sucked him down her throat as far as he would go. It was easy to suck a dick his size. She didn't have to work hard. Soon after beginning, she felt his hands cradle the back of her head. He thrust his hips and started fucking her mouth. He moaned when she cupped his balls and squeezed. That was when she stopped. There was no way she would allow him to shoot off in her mouth. The night would end too quickly if she allowed that.

She stood up but kept stroking his dick. He tried to kiss her lips. She turned her head away. "No kissing. Take me to your bed."

She didn't have to tell him twice. He twisted his hand in his pants to keep them up and yanked her through the house and up the stairs. In the upstairs corridor, they passed one closed door at the top of the stairs. She made out the silhouette of a toilet facing her in a dark bathroom at the end of the hall. There were two more doors adjacent to each other.

The door on the left stood wide open when they approached it. No light was on inside the room. Lacy squinted inside and saw Rich lying naked on his back just inside the doorway. Bunny was naked too and sat on top of him with her chest against his while cradling his head in her arms to keep him still. Her fat, white ass bounced up and down as she fucked him. Rich's hands gripped her pale behind as she rode. She fucked him so hard that it looked like Rich couldn't handle it and he was trying to slow her down.

Dame stopped to watch. Her long red hair crawled down her back like flames. She cupped her huge titties and squeezed the life out of them, then looked over at Dame staring at her as she rode Rich harder.

"Goddamn you got some good pussy," Rich declared, reaching up to squeeze her breasts.

Lacy grabbed Dame's hand and pulled him close to the other room. "Is this your bedroom?"

Dame nodded. "Yeah."

Lacy closed the door once they made it in. Dame's bedroom was a nice one. He had a matching black lacquered bedroom set. His clothes were neat in the closet. And the room smelled clean. Unlike some men's rooms that she'd been in.

She pushed him on the bed. "Take off your clothes."

Dame squirmed to shimmy out of his pants as Lacy pulled off her top. "Damn you got some nice titties," he said, stroking his skinny dick.

Lacy glanced at the open closet. She saw ten or twelve boxes of Jordan's.

Once she was naked, she lay on the bed beside Dame. He still had his boxers on.

He rolled on top of her and kissed trails down to her belly. "You don't have to do that," she told him.

He ignored her. Next thing she knew, he had her legs spread wide and his tongue splitting her apart. He ate her pussy with all the amateur techniques that she hated. He licked her outer lips, sometimes stuck his tongue in the pussy, and ignored her yearning clitoris all together. Determined to get some kind of nut out of the deal, she grabbed the back of his head and grinded her clit into his nose to stimulate it. Soon after, her moans echoed in the room and she felt her orgasm building.

Dame's phone chimed.

He pulled back and looked for the sound.

"Call them back," Lacy said. She laid on the bed with her legs wide. Her fingers rolled around her clit as she tried to keep herself hot and ready.

Dame found his phone on the floor and picked it up to look at the number. "Damn!" Dame shot off a text. "I told this nigga to wait."

"You comin' back to bed?" Lacy asked him.

"Gimmie a minute. My man is at the front door."

Dame stepped into his pants and then hurried to the closet. Lacy rolled onto her side and watched him pull up a corner of the carpet. She heard wood clanking against wood. Then Dame came out of the closet holding a plastic grocery bag with something wrapped tight inside.

He stopped by the bed long enough to look down on Lacy's naked body and said, "I promise I'll be right back. I just need two minutes." Dame rushed out of the bedroom.

Across the hall, Lacy saw Bunny lying on her side, still on the floor. Rich laid behind her, hoisting one of her legs in the air as he plowed into her. Lacy made out his balls slapping Bunny's soft white flesh. Rich had a big dick. It was long, thick and black sliding in and out of Bunny. Yet Bunny lie there looking bored, as if she didn't feel a thing.

Bunny moaned, "Yeah, fuck me in my ass. Do it. Deeper. Oh. Fuck my ass with that big black dick." Her eyes met Lacy's and she silently gestured for Lacy to get moving.

Lacy hopped out of the bed and hurried to the closet where Dame had knelt down. She pressed around on the floor until she felt a loose floorboard beneath the carpet. She pulled up a corner of the carpet, then jimmied out the floorboard with her fingernail, revealing a gaping hole where the floorboard had come from. She leaned over and peered inside. Lacy saw rolls and rolls of banded bills and another grocery bag. She pulled out the grocery bag. It was some kind of dope. Coke? Heroin? She didn't have time to find out.

Instead of taking the dope and money, Lacy replaced the bag and wedged the floorboard back where it belonged. She rolled the carpet back to its original position so that it looked untouched, then she climbed back into bed to wait for Dame to return.

He never came back.

She heard an explosion, then gunfire. Lacy scrambled to put on her clothes as a parade of boots stomped up the stairs. She looked up just in time to see three men in black rush at her with assault rifles drawn. "DEA! On the fucking floor! Now Bitch!"

SIX

ROCHELLE HURRIED INTO THE ENTRANCE of Queen of Spades Gentleman's Club at a quarter past midnight. Darla, the mixed door girl, threw her a quizzical glance as she walked into the foyer.

Darla pulled down her glittery facemask and whispered, "Rochelle, where have you been? Roscoe has been on a tirade all night. And now you walk in here an hour late."

Rochelle kept her mask over her face, but paused long enough to say, "I had shit to do. Roscoe can get mad all he wants. I'm always here when I'm supposed to be. Being late one time won't make the world stop moving."

Darla rolled her eyes and let her mask cover her mouth again. "Oh-kay."

Rochelle walked through the double doors leading into the interior of the club. Queen of Spades was as spacious as an arena with three major stages and two minor ones. All of the patrons and dancers sat at safe social distances and wore facemasks, as dictated by the mayor's executive order. Because of coronavirus, the club was filled to half-capacity, meaning the dancers had to work harder for the few dollars they made. Water sculptures lined the back wall of the main stage, where Cotton hung upside down from a pole by the crook behind one knee. She twerked her ass in circles as a crowd of men tossed dollar bills on the stage to the banging beat of Two Chains' "All I Want for My Birthday". Rochelle passed a neon sign directing club goers to the Champagne Room at the back, guarded by two burly black men wearing bright yellow T-shirts with SECURITY written in bold black across their massive chests and yellow facemasks.

Rochelle glanced up at Cotton and noticed her roommate staring seductively at her from across the dark club. The gaze unnerved Rochelle, even from so far away. She turned her back to the stage and headed toward the main bar at the front of the club. Only one bartender, Juicy, made drinks when Rochelle stepped behind the bar.

Juicy had three glasses on the counter in front of her as she struggled to make the drinks. She looked up to Rochelle as she neared. "Girl, where have you been? We are busy as hell tonight." Her voice was muffled behind a black mask speckled with rhinestones.

Rochelle put her bag on the floor and picked up an apron. She frowned at the sweat beading on Juicy's forehead. "I had to take care of something. Sorry. What do you have that I can do?"

Juicy shook her head and pointed to a stack of tickets stabbed on a spike in the center of the counter. "All those."

Rochelle didn't complain about the work. She grabbed a few tickets and started making drinks as fast as she could. She didn't notice Roscoe behind her until he cleared his throat. She turned around abruptly. "Don't be walking up behind me, Roscoe."

He crossed his arms over his wide chest. "This is my goddamn club. I'll walk where the fuck I want."

Roscoe was an ex-con who had served fifteen years for murder in North Carolina. He stood at least six 'three, with a smooth, black, bald head dented with scars from fights and assaults. His massive chest and biceps were a testament to the time he spent behind bars. Roscoe owned the building, but his wife, an ex-stripper named Anastasia, owned the liquor license. Anastasia had hired Rochelle, not Roscoe, so Rochelle didn't fear his empty threats, even though she did fear his scrutiny.

"Where you been?" he asked her. "Juicy been busting her ass waiting on you to come in. This isn't like you. What you got going on that I should know about?"

Rochelle smirked, knowing that Roscoe only wanted her there so he could sneak Juicy off to his office and bust her ass while his wife Anastasia was at home watching their four kids.

Rochelle ignored his anger. "I had something to take care of, Roscoe. It won't happen again."

"It better not. And what the fuck are you wearing? Niggas come here to see naked bitches. Jeans? They can see a bitch like you're dressed at the crib. Why spend money for that?"

Rochelle looked at her clothes. She wore tight jeans and a plain black sweatshirt. She looked at Juicy, who wore gold booty shorts and a bra so sparse that she may as well not have anything on at all. Her own bartending uniform was in her bag.

"I just got here. I'll go change." She turned to leave, all too happy to get away from him.

Roscoe grabbed Rochelle's arm to stop her. "Wait. Change later. Juicy needs a break. She's been working her ass off." He looked to Juicy. "Come on, Juicy. I need you to handle something in the back."

Juicy shook her head. "I—I can't right now. I'm busy."

Roscoe's fists clenched. "Fuck you say, bitch? I need you to handle something in the back. It ain't a choice. Get your motherfucking ass in the office. Now."

Juicy dropped what she was doing and followed Roscoe. When she passed Rochelle, Rochelle muttered, "Yeah. Go handle that."

Juicy sucked her teeth. "I will. Jealous bitch."

She watched Juicy and Roscoe make their way through the club toward his office. *Ain't nothing to be jealous about.* Roscoe tried her when she first started working, like he tried all the girls. Most were too stupid to say no. They gave in, thinking they had to fuck to get ahead. They didn't realize that not fucking him was their true power. By not giving in, he would always respect them. He may talk shit to Rochelle, but he respected her, and respect was worth fighting for.

She finished the stack of drink orders just as a few of the waitresses were bringing more, but she was caught up enough to handle the new ones. Cotton walked over wearing a black one-piece with a thong back. Her sheer black facemask allowed an admirer to view her face while she was still protected from the virus. Her blonde afro was freshly picked and soft, like a cotton ball. She sat on a stool in front of Rochelle. Rochelle tried to ignore her.

Cotton watched Rochelle making drinks. "You mad at me about this morning?"

Rochelle didn't look up. "No."

Cotton waited a moment before saying, "I love you, Rochelle. You know that. And I know that you don't like girls in that way. It's okay. You don't have to commit to me. I just want to have a little fun every once in a while. You haven't been with a man in a long time."

"That's by choice."

"I know, Rochelle. And if you had a man, I could live with that too. Just don't shut me out. Okay? I need you."

Rochelle looked into Cotton's eyes and knew that she would give in at some point. She loved Cotton too. Part of her resistance was based on her own feelings. She liked making love to Cotton, but she didn't want to be with a woman. Cotton said that she could have sex with no relationship, but for Cotton, having sex was a gateway drug to a relationship. Rochelle thought that in Cotton's mind, it would start with regular sex. Once Rochelle got used to Cotton eating her pussy, she'd beg her for a relationship. Cotton was worse than a man in that regard. She tried to entice Rochelle with little lies to get what she wanted.

"I don't want that, Cotton."

Cotton stared at her for a moment. She rolled her eyes. "Make me a Hennessey. No ice."

Rochelle stopped what she was doing to make the drink just so Cotton could get out of her face.

After Rochelle slid the drink in front of her, Cotton asked, "Why were you late? By the way."

Rochelle paused for the first time since she'd walked in the door. She knew that Cotton was disappointed in her, but they were friends before they were anything else. Cotton was the only person that Rochelle could share her problems with. "I had to go to the fucking police station to pick up Lacy."

"What?!"

"Girl, yes. She and Bunny were at some niggas house when the police raided it. One of them had a shootout with the police. They shot him, but he's still alive. He's laid up in the hospital half dead. The boy ain't but fifteen years old. I told Lacy that it should have been her dumb ass all shot up. That's the only way she'll listen to anybody."

Cotton stood up from her stool. "What were they doing there? They could have been killed."

"Chasing behind some no-good ass nigga's. They found a quarter kilo of cocaine on the guy they shot. I think they found some money in the house, but not much."

"I'm surprised they let them two young, dumb bitches go.."

Rochelle nodded. "Me too. The one they shot admitted that they had only met Lacy and Bunny that night. He claimed the drugs too. The police had to let them go."

"They got lucky."

"*Lacy* got lucky. Bunny's mama, Becky, showed up about the same time that I did. *With* her little boyfriend."

"The short nigga that thinks he's a pimp? What's his name? Rudy?"

"Mm-hm. They walked in there looking like they weighed fifteen pounds apiece. Becky's titties were the biggest things on her, and they look like they shrunk a couple sizes. When the cops brought Bunny out, Becky acted like mom of the year. She was hollering and yelling. She punched Bunny right there in the middle of the police station. In the damn eye!"

Cotton winced. "The police didn't try to stop her?"

Rochelle shook her head sadly. "I wish they had. The cop I was talking to said he wished more parents smacked their kids around. It might keep them out of the police station in the first place." Rochelle frowned. "They don't know what Bunny's been through *all because of her mama*. Most of the time she got punched for nothing. At least she did something wrong this time."

Cotton shook her head. "White people get away with everything." Cotton sat back down. "If they knew what her mom's ex-boyfriend did to her . . . and that Becky knew about it the whole time and didn't say anything . . ."

"They would have arrested her on the spot," Rochelle finished.

"I feel bad for Bunny."

"Me too," Rochelle admitted. "But she's nineteen years old. She can leave anytime she wants to. It's not my responsibility to take care of her. Besides, I don't have the money to take care of her even if I wanted to."

Cotton didn't respond. She sat in her own thoughts while staring into her drink, looking like she had lost the urge to finish it.

Rochelle started making drinks again, but she allowed her eyes to roam around the club. At the back, in the VIP section, she spotted a group of men throwing stacks of money toward two dancers on all fours in front of them. She noticed one of the men sitting on the couch alone. The guy was light-skinned with good hair. He said nothing as the men around him whooped and hollered. He sat away from everyone else and had his mask pulled down over his chin. He stared at the girls, but he didn't indulge in the festivities.

Rochelle asked Cotton, "Who's that?"

Cotton followed her gaze. "Some nigga. I think his name is Devon."

Rochelle watched him reach into a bag and pull out a stack of bills. Instead of throwing them himself, he handed the money to a man on his team. Rochelle knew he was the boss of that little clique from the way he moved. She asked Cotton. "Why didn't you find out what he's got going on? He might be balling."

Cotton swirled her drink in the glass. "I was worried about you, baby. I been thinking about you all day. I didn't want you mad at me. Shit. I can't think of anything but your sweet ass."

Rochelle rolled her eyes. "We've got bills to pay."

"I know I should have been on him, but I . . ."

"Go over there," Rochelle said. "See what he's about."

Cotton looked her in the eye for a moment before standing and adjusting her breasts. "Okay. Can we talk about . . . about us . . . later tonight?"

Rochelle nodded. "Maybe not tonight. But we'll talk. I'm not ready yet."

Rochelle watched Cotton walk toward the VIP section. She threw an extra twist in her hips as she neared. Cotton didn't walk straight up to the guy, but she slowed down enough to grab his attention as she walked past. Rochelle noticed Devon perk up. He snapped his fingers to get his man's attention and pulled his mask up to whisper something to him. Not long after, Cotton was being escorted up the stairs to a spot at Devon's side. Twenty minutes later, Cotton was leading Devon to the

Champagne Room. Rochelle smiled to herself, hoping they were going to get paid well tonight.

SEVEN

COTTON ACTUALLY LIKED DEVON. He was smooth and genuine. She hadn't fallen for a man in a long time, but if she had to fall for one, she could definitely see herself falling for a guy like him. He had the kind of appeal that attracted her. In a way, she kind of wanted to learn more about him. Just to see if she could really like him, but she didn't have time. And after tonight, he would never want to see her again, unless she was lying in a coffin.

She followed his white Cadillac Escalade to Buckhead in her BMW. It was a nice house. Much larger than she had expected. He pulled into the three-car garage and threw his hand out of the window to gesture for her to pull in as well. Cotton parked beside his car. The garage door slowly closed behind her.

Before getting out, Cotton sent Devon's address and a description of his house to Rochelle. She hadn't wanted to park in the garage because it would be easier for Rochelle to find the house if she saw her white BMW out front, but life was full of surprises, and they would have to improvise. As she was opening the door, she received a text from Rochelle: *got it*

Devon stepped to her side of the car and looked at the phone in her hand. "What are you doing?"

"Checking the time."

He helped her out of the car. "What time is it?"

"A little after three," she replied, hoping she passed his little test.

He took her in his arms as soon as she got out and kissed her hard. Cotton's back pressed against her car, wishing he would slow down some. In the Champagne Room earlier, she had taken him into a back booth later on, far away from the bouncers, and he was a different person. Around his people, he'd been almost cold. He smiled very little and showed no signs that he was enjoying himself. He'd acted as a leader.

Alone with Cotton, he loosened up. She didn't kiss him, but she allowed him to touch her in places that she wouldn't allow anyone else as she danced for him. When time was up, she reached into her garter and handed the bouncer another twenty to let him stay.

"You like me, don't you?" he'd asked.

"I love power," she'd replied. "And that's what you are. Power in its rarest form."

That comment made him look at her with a hunger she'd never seen in a man.

Minutes later, she had his dick in her mouth. His dick wasn't unusually large and delicious. She liked him enough to give him some good head. She enjoyed pleasing him. The bouncer came back just before he finished and told her that their time was up. Devon was furious. He offered more money, but Cotton explained that a customer could only get one session. They were lucky to have squeezed two out. Cotton let down her guard and kissed him then. It was a daring thing to do with corona and all types of other diseases floating around. After that, she promised to let him finish in her mouth later that night . . . if he wanted to hook up after the club closed.

And so they stood in his garage at a quarter past three kissing the morning away. Cotton wore a loose white skirt and a black silk blouse. Devon's hand dipped beneath her skirt and his fingers slipped past her thong to fondle her soaking wet pussy. Cotton moaned when she was supposed to. She rubbed the back of his head and kissed his neck. She whispered that she wanted him and let him put his hands wherever he desired.

Through a garage window, she spotted a set of headlights driving down Devon's street. He was so busy fingering her that he didn't notice. The car parked up the street. Seconds later, the headlights blinked off.

Cotton pushed him away gently. "You got a bed or something? I don't want to do it out here in the garage."

Devon came to his senses. Follow me."

They entered the house through a door leading into the kitchen. Devon's phone rang as soon as they made it inside. He looked at the caller ID and said, "I gotta take this."

Cotton snapped her fingers. "I left something in my car."

Before answering the phone, he said, "Go get it. I'll be in the living room." He answered the phone. "What up, Papi? I've been waiting on you to call all day."

Cotton hurried back into the garage and unlocked a side door. As she walked back into the house, she sent a text to Rochelle reading: *garage door*

Devon was still on the phone when she entered the living room. The room was decorated for Christmas, complete with a large tree, donning dozens of presents beneath. Mistletoe hung from every doorway leading into the room.

"That's not enough," he said into the phone. "He'll pay eleven apiece or he can eat the tip of my dick. Yeah. That's right. Eleven. I'll meet him first thing in the morning. And he better have the money. Cash. Who the fuck do you think you're dealing with. Eight a.m.? I'll be there."

Cotton sat on the couch and watched him, noting that he came across as the vain type of man who enjoyed giving girls a glimpse of his business life by holding conversations on the phone in front of them—a weakness in her eyes, but a weakness that served her purposes. At least she knew how much money he was working with.

Devon hung up the phone and sat on the couch next to her. He draped his arm across her shoulder. "Sorry about that."

"It's okay," she said. "Do you need me to leave? Sounds like you've got a meeting in the morning."

He kissed her on the neck. "Nah, baby. You can stay the night. I don't have to leave until ten minutes before eight."

To Cotton, that meant the money was somewhere in the house. Her heart picked up pace in her chest.

Devon kissed her on the lips. She allowed it and felt her nipples stiffen. His fingers gently opened her blouse, revealing a sheer black bra beneath. Cotton rubbed her palm over his chest, then allowed her hand to slip between his legs. She felt something hard down there that was not his dick. He moved her hand away.

"Get on the floor," he told her.

"You wanna go upstairs?" she asked.

"No. I want to do it here."

Cotton stood and pulled off her shirt. She started to unbutton her skirt when Devon took her in his arms.

He whispered, "Leave it on for now." He pulled her down to the carpeted floor in front of the Christmas tree, positioning her on all fours. "That's it." She felt his hands lifting her skirt up and over the mounds of her behind. "Damn, look at that fat ass." His fingers stroked her pussy roughly. "I was thinking about fucking you from the back all night. I saw you on stage, and I knew I had to fuck you. I was waiting for you all night."

Devon pulled her panties to the side and slipped his finger inside of her. From the corner of her eye, she saw him place a black automatic on the floor beside them. She thought that she could reach it if she had to, but she wasn't sure. She hoped she wouldn't have to try.

Devon wasted no time pushing his hard dick into her. His hands gripped her hips as he fucked her. Cotton's fingers gripped the carpet. She hadn't been fucked by a man in over a year. Although she didn't miss the machismo attitudes of men she dated in the past, she did miss the feeling of being filled up by a long, hard dick. A woman could never replace that feeling.

She opened her eyes and looked at the Christmas tree. She was closer to it than she thought. Cotton made out Devon poised behind her in the skewed reflection of a gold Christmas ornament. His eyes were closed. His face was contorted in a mask of pleasure that only good pussy could induce.

She stared deeper into the reflection and spotted a dark figure creeping into the room from the kitchen doorway. The figure held a pistol pointed up as they tiptoed closer. Cotton reached between her legs and gripped Devon's balls tightly as he fucked her.

"Oh, shit," he moaned. "That's it. Rub my balls."

All the while, the dark figure crept closer. The figure raised the pistol, ready to bash Devon over the head.

Through the Christmas ornament, Cotton saw him open his eyes and lock onto the figure behind him by looking in the same reflection that she was.

"What the fuck?" He rolled away and reached for his gun.

Cotton was faster. Her hand darted out and reached too, but her fingers failed to grip the pistol's butt. Instead, she merely pushed it farther away from them both. Devon and Cotton's eyes met for a split second before he went for the gun again. In his gaze, she recognized a silent accusation of betrayal—betrayal along with the promise of vengeance. She scurried to the gun beside him, knowing that if she didn't get there first, she would die.

Their shoulders bumped as they scrambled to get there. Devon's hand grabbed the barrel. Cotton's grabbed the butt. He jerked his arm and shoved his elbow into her mouth in an attempt to push her away. Cotton held on for dear life, knowing her survival depended on it.

Rochelle stepped closer and aimed the pistol down at the back of Devon's head. "Let go of the gun!" she shouted to him.

"Kill me, bitch!" he shouted, cocking back and punching Cotton in the side of the head.

Rochelle followed Devon with her pistol, wanting to shoot him, but too afraid to miss and hit Cotton. "Let it go!"

"Bitch, do you know who I am?" Devon threw all his weight onto Cotton and forced her to let go of the gun. He fumbled with it until he got a good grip and pressed the barrel to Cotton's head as he lay on top of her. He turned back long enough to look up into Rochelle's eyes. "You put your gun down, and . . ."

Rochelle fired a shot into his back. The bullet ripped through his side and exited as quickly as it entered, lodging in the floor just beside Cotton. Devon dropped the gun and rolled off, howling in pain.

"You shot me! You crazy bitch!"

Rochelle walked closer and stomped on his neck. "I'mma shoot your dumb-ass again if you don't shut the fuck up. Don't play with me. I don't give a fuck about you."

Cotton picked up Devon's pistol and held it at his face, still trembling from having it pointed at her. "I ought to kill you, motherfucker."

"Calm down," Rochelle told her. "We didn't come here for that."

"He was going to kill me," Cotton complained.

"Not now," Rochelle added. "Nobody is going to die now."

Devon tried to sit up, but he stayed on the ground once he realized the pain was too great. "I need an ambulance. I'm going to die if I don't see a doctor."

Rochelle shook her head. "You're going to die if you don't tell me where the money is."

"What money?"

"He's got money," Cotton said. "I heard him talking on the phone. He's got to have a lot."

Devon pointed at Cotton. "I'mma kill you bitch!"

Rochelle jarred her foot harder into his neck. "You want to live? Where's the money."

Devon laid back down and blinked at the ceiling. Rochelle could tell that he was in a lot of pain. His silence told her that he was deciding what to do. "Goddamn!" He hissed. "Upstairs. In a safe. In my bedroom closet."

Cotton crawled close to him, baring her fangs, pressing the barrel of the gun tight against his temple. "What's the combination?"

Devon winced. "It's unlocked. Ain't nobody stupid enough to rob me . . ." He stared off into space, looking like he was thinking about what he'd just said. "The motherfuckers that rob me will have hell to pay. Everybody knows that."

Rochelle ignored his threat. She looked to Cotton. "Go get it."

Cotton stood up, wanting to shoot him before walking away, but she lowered the gun to her side and hurried out of the room.

Devon peered up at Rochelle. "You don't know who I am."

"I don't care who you are."

"If you let me live, I won't do anything to anybody. I'll tell my people some niggas robbed me and I don't know who they were. Just take the money and call an ambulance. Please." A trickle of a tear cascaded from his eye.

Rochelle looked at the doorway where Cotton had disappeared and wondered what was taking her so long. "Shut the fuck up." She glanced back to him. The pool of blood around his body grew wider and darker. She stepped away to make sure it didn't touch her.

Devon also noticed the pool of blood. He sobbed uncontrollably now. "Don't let me die," he begged. "Please. I got two kids. They need me. I won't tell anybody about you. I swear."

She looked down on him again, disgusted at his pleading. She thought it was sad to see a man beg for his life. Especially when she was sure that he had killed someone else. She wondered if he had given them a chance to survive. Probably not. And if they let him go, he would kill someone else. It was a sure bet. Hustlers all promised the same things when they had a pistol pointed at their head.

Cotton came running back into the room carrying a Gucci valise in one hand and Devon's gun in the other. She hurried to Rochelle and pulled open the bag. It was stuffed with banded bills. "There was drugs too," she told Rochelle, "But I didn't mess with that."

"Good," Rochelle responded. She looked to Devon. "You got anything else?"

"Not here," he admitted, sniffling. "But I've got a lot more somewhere else. I'll tell you, if you help me." Then he asked, "Are you going to call an ambulance?"

Rochelle didn't reply. She took the valise from Cotton's hand and started walking toward the kitchen and the garage door where she had entered. She made it inside the garage and paused on the steps with her eyes focused on the concrete floor.

Devon continued begging after Rochelle walked away, "Please. No. Don't. I wasn't going to hurt you. I . . ."

Six quick gunshots echoed in the garage. She heard nothing after that.

Rochelle had not planned on killing Devon, but they'd fucked up. The plan was for Rochelle to pistol whip him, tie him and Cotton up, then force him to tell her where the money was. That way Cotton would be absolved of any guilt. But they'd blown that chance.

He knew Cotton had set him up. There was no way he would let her live. And he might torture her to find out Rochelle's identity. The only way to make it right, was to make sure he couldn't talk or seek revenge. Sometimes they didn't do what they wanted to do. They did what they had to. Death was a risk in their business.

But the sad part is they'd never had to kill anyone before. Devon was the first.

EIGHT

THE EMS VAN WAS BLOCKING THE ENTRANCE to Devon's house when Marco pulled up at half-past six in the morning. Cops were out in full force, combing the lawn for evidence, exiting the house with taped-up boxes and a laptop. Some neighbors stood on their lawns wearing robes, slippers, and facemasks. Marco parked two houses down and stared at the flashing lights and commotion. This was the last place he wanted to show his face at—the last place he should be showing his face.

Marco strapped a facemask over his nose and mouth, then he pulled a white toboggan down over the top of his head, hoping it masked his identity enough to get in and get out without being noticed. He climbed out of his Mercedes and yanked his bomber jacket a little tighter to fight the cold December morning.

Two white uniformed cops stood on Devon's front lawn behind a stripe of CAUTION tape tied to two trees. Marco approached the tape and tried to duck beneath it. One of the cops rushed over and pushed him in the chest, warning, "Stay back!" As he reached for his pistol, Marco reached for his pistol too. The cop reached for his too. They drew at the same time, both locked, loaded, and ready to shoot.

"Hold on, Smith!" A voice called out. "He's one of ours."

From the corner of his eye, Marco spotted Detective Jack Blake hurrying across the lawn toward them. The cop didn't lower his pistol, so neither did Marco. "Shoot me," he hissed to the uniformed cop. "That's all you want to do is kill a nigga anyway. Go ahead. You better kill me. 'Cause if you don't . . ."

The cop huffed, "Fuck you."

And then Blake was on him, pressing his pale palm on the officer's gun to force him to lower it. "Smith, I just said he was one of ours. You pulling out on cops now?"

Officer Smith turned to Blake. "He's not wearing a badge."

Blake ran a shaky hand through his blond hair. He glanced at Marco. "Where's your shield?"

Marco lowered his gun and smirked toward Officer Smith. He reached into his jacket and pulled out his badge, letting it dangle over his belly from the end of a long Cuban-link gold chain. "He didn't give me a chance to pull it out. Motherfucker so fast to pull out on a black man."

"Hey!" Smith retorted. "You could've been anybody."

Marco nodded as he placed his gun back in his waistband. "Anybody black."

"Fuck you!" Smith spat.

"No, fuck with me. That's what you do. I'd love to put some of this marksmanship training to work."

Blake stepped between them. "Okay. Okay. That's enough. Marco, come on, let's go. I've got something to show you." He wrapped his arm around Marco's shoulder and led him toward Devon's house. When they were out of earshot, Blake whispered, "You've got to take it easy on these guys, Marco. When it all comes down, a guy like Smith will be the only one watching your back. Think about it."

"Fuck him and his mama too. I don't need a clown like him watching my back."

"This isn't a one-man show, Marco. Have you been with those dealers so long that you think you're untouchable? Do I need to have you brought in?"

Marco pushed away from Blake. "Are you fucking serious? I've been trying to get in with Genesis for three years now. I've spent time in jail trying to get next to him. I don't see my family. If you pull me out now, I'll have nothing to show for everything I've sacrificed."

Blake bounded up the steps leading to Devon's front door. "Act like it."

Marco stood at the bottom of the stairs and looked up at Devon's house, wondering how Devon had a bigger home than Genesis, the man he sold drugs for. "I shouldn't be here, Blake."

Blake shrugged and walked inside. Marco had no choice but to follow his supervisor. His eyes were drawn to a chandelier just inside the foyer. Marco wasn't sure if it was crystal or not. He wasn't cultured enough to know the difference between plain glass and expensive glass, nor did he care to be. He held no ambition for luxury.

Marco had grown up poor in Macon, Georgia. He never owned a pair of Jordan's as a kid, and never thought to ask for them. His mother couldn't afford expensive shoes working as a maid in a rundown hotel. She could barely keep food on the table for him and his older brother, Chauncey.

Marco followed Blake into the living room where two other detectives hunched over a huge bloodstain in the center of the floor, right in front of a Christmas tree. Seeing that drying blood made him think of his brother Chauncey even more. Chauncey had expensive ambitions—ambitions that killed him, just like someone had killed Devon.

Blake stared at the detectives working. "Victim's name was Devon . . ."

"Wright," Marco finished for him.

Blake kept his eyes on the murder scene. "Figured you knew him."

Marco nodded. "He was Genesis' right hand. Smooth motherfucker. Like a blade on ice. I just saw him last night."

"When Jamal Washington was killed?"

Marco nodded, remembering how Devon had stood over Jamal's body unloading shots. From the looks of multiple bullet holes in the carpet, someone had done the same to him.

Karma was a bitch that didn't think twice. Hadn't taken her long to catch up this time. Not long at all.

Blake looked to Marco. "I know you're in deep with these guys, but now isn't the time to hold back."

"I was debriefed about Jamal Washington this morning. I turned in my cellphone for GPS tracking and bought another one. Internal Affairs didn't even blink. I've been cleared, pending further investigation. I don't have shit to hide. If you want to ask me a question, ask it."

Blake nodded. "Do you think this murder is connected to the Washington killing last night?"

Marco thought about the pretty girl he'd seen Jamal with the night before. The Latina beauty Butterscotch. She was the only close contact he'd known Jamal to have, and he didn't recognize a killer instinct in her eyes. "I don't have a clue. I mean, it could be, but I don't know. These guys aren't choir boys. They make more enemies than friends. Is that why you called me out here? You could've asked me that on the phone."

"Not quite." Blake reached into his jacket pocket and pulled out his phone. "We don't have much to go on. Whoever did this was a professional."

"Now you're saying Genesis hired someone to hit Devon? That doesn't make sense. I've been with them both, and I didn't get that at all."

"No, I'm not saying a professional killer. A professional robber." Blake played a grainy, black and white surveillance video on his phone. "We got this from the neighbor's security cameras. The quality is fucked up, but . . ."

Marco squinted at the screen. A car parked on the street. Moments later, a figure wearing all black climbed out. It was hard to make out, but he swore the figure was wearing a ski mask. The figure crept off on foot out of the shot, leaving the car. "Anybody get a license plate?"

Blake shook his head. "I wish. I'd be at home eating waffles with my daughter right now if it was that easy. Best we could get was a sixteen-year-old kid who claims he was on the phone with his girlfriend when the car parked on the street. He said he thinks the car was burgundy."

"That's not a lot to go on."

"It's not," Blake admitted. "That's why I called you out here. I was hoping you could point me in the right direction. Maybe you've seen someone around him that was driving a burgundy car?"

Marco shook his head. "They don't let me into their personal lives. So far, it's just business."

Blake watched him for a minute, then he fast-forwarded the surveillance footage. "We got this twenty minutes after the burgundy car showed up."

The dark figure sprinted back into the shot and hurried to get into the car. Marco noticed the person carrying a small bag. He hadn't noticed them carrying a bag before. The car started and pulled off without turning on the headlights. Seconds later, another car drove up the street behind the burgundy car.

Blake paused the footage just as the second car was on the middle of the screen. "That's a white BMW."

"Model? License plate?"

Blake shook his head.

Marco almost laughed. "You ain't got shit."

Blake lowered his phone. "Did you see that bag? We searched the house already. Found a kilo and a half of coke in a safe upstairs. Safe was wide open. But guess what? No cash. We tore the place up. Not one red cent."

"That's all they came for. It wasn't about revenge for Jamal Washington's death. They obviously aren't drug dealers. They knew he had money and killed him for it."

"Maybe," Blake said. "A thief would have taken the dope too. They deliberately left the drugs. That says they're not desperate. They can pick and choose what they want. That's why I think they're pros. Maybe they're freelancers. Maybe they're Blood Gang members. I don't know. But they've done this type of thing before."

Marco no longer wondered why Blake called him out there. "Which makes you think they'll strike again."

Blake nodded. "Maybe at your boy, Genesis. Not too many people get close to the big man. This guy Devon, he was right up there with Genesis. Watch your back. You might be next. These guys are climbing the ladder of success, and there's no telling who they'll step on to get to the top."

NINE

ROCHELLE HEARD THE SOBBING through Cotton's bedroom door as she walked past to go to the bathroom. She paused in the hallway, listening. She closed her eyes and saw Devon squirming on the floor with a bullet hole flowering blood across his back. The memory was enough to make her want to cry, but she didn't. She opened her eyes and walked into the bathroom.

Cotton was still crying when she came out. She paused in front of Cotton's door, knowing that there wasn't much that she could say. Cotton had killed a man. Not because she wanted to, but because she had to. What words would take that pain away? Rochelle could think of none. Yet she felt her fist knocking. She listened and heard no response.

"Cotton?"

"I'm okay."

Rochelle pushed the door open and poked her head inside. Cotton was wrapped in a ball on her bed. Only a thin bedsheet covered her. She kept her face to the far wall, away from the door.

"I said I'm okay, Rochelle."

Rochelle stepped into the room wearing only an oversized T-shirt and panties. It was early morning. She'd been up all night long. How could she sleep after what had happened? She didn't need someone to talk to, but she suspected that Cotton did, regardless of what she said.

Rochelle sat on the edge of Cotton's bed and looked down on her friend and roommate. They'd known each other since they were in middle school. Had never spent more than a day or two apart. When they lived separately, they always hung out. They shared clothes, boyfriends, and growing pains. She would do anything for Cotton. Well . . . almost anything.

"It's not your fault, Cotton."

"I know—I just—I don't feel right."

Rochelle scooted her legs onto the bed and laid down beside her. "I would be worried about you if you did feel right."

Cotton was quiet for a long time. She sniffled a bit, then said, "Remember when your mom died and the bank kicked you and Lacy out of your house?"

Rochelle wished that she could forget. She had no job. No way to pay the three-thousand dollars her mom owed. Because her mom had been murdered, the insurance company would not honor her life insurance policy, and Rochelle and Lacy were left homeless and penniless. After sleeping in a shelter for one night, Rochelle weighed her options. She could sell drugs, sell her ass, or rob dudes to get the money they needed. Cotton was dancing even back then and had her own apartment. As a last resort, Rochelle showed up on Cotton's doorstep with an idea.

"I remember," she said. "We robbed that dude you met at Wendy's."

Cotton giggled a little. The sound was a welcome change from her grief.

Cotton said, "The one in the purple Cadillac. He had finger waves and rocked those lime green gators."

Rochelle smiled some. "Don't talk shit. I got three-hundred for those green gators. We ate for a month after that."

"He was the first one."

"He was," Rochelle said. He was an easy lick. An older guy. Cotton gave him head behind a dumpster in the Wendy's parking lot. Rochelle ran up on the driver's side door with her mom's Lorcin 380. Rochelle didn't know who was more afraid, her or him. He offered to take them back to his house and give them everything he had. Rochelle was too afraid to think about going to his house. She told him that what he had in his pockets was enough. That's how new they were to the game. She asked Cotton, "Do you wish we would have stopped after him?"

Cotton lie silent in thought. "I don't know. We bought this house. We've got two cars. What else would we have done?" She looked off into space, no doubt thinking of Devon and what happened to him the night before. "This is what we do."

Rochelle could not recall all the men they had robbed over the years. There were too many to count. They had pistol whipped them. Tied them up. Rochelle shot one in the leg. But they had never killed anyone. Not until last night. Killing a lick was always something she thought would happen eventually but tried to avoid it at all costs. She went into every job knowing that this could be the guy to resist. They'd been lucky for years.

Well . . . that luck had run out.

She scooted in close and wrapped her arms around Cotton's middle. Through the sheet, she could tell that Cotton was naked. She couldn't remember a time when Cotton had slept with clothes on, even as a young girl. Cotton's hands grasped Rochelle's and pulled them close to her chest. Rochelle felt Cotton's heart thumping like a bass drum in her chest. The sun beamed in through the window, bathing Cotton in white light, making her blonde mane glow like a halo.

Tears flowed from Cotton's green eyes again, making them resemble shards of polished jade. "I'm sorry that I messed up," she said. "I should have reached for the gun faster. He shouldn't have overpowered me like that."

Rochelle pulled her tighter. "It's okay. We can't take it back. I'm just as guilty as you."

Slowly Cotton turned in Rochelle's grasp to face her. Their eyes locked. "I love you, Rochelle. I would die if anything happened to you."

Rochelle's hands stroked up and down Cotton's back. "I love you too."

She kissed Cotton on the forehead. Afterward, their faces remained close. She stared into Cotton's eyes as Cotton kissed her on the forehead. Rochelle only wanted to dry Cotton's tears. She had no intentions of starting something. But when Cotton kissed her again—on the lips—Rochelle didn't have the energy to turn away. Her mouth opened and accepted Cotton's tongue when it was offered. Cotton's breath was warm and stale, but not tart. She greedily sucked Rochelle's tongue, as if she'd been waiting for this moment, couldn't believe it had finally arrived, and was determined to cherish every second of it.

Cotton's hands roamed beneath Rochelle's nightshirt, grabbing handfuls of Rochelle's ass and thighs with each grip. Rochelle was no innocent party. She pulled away the bedsheet and found Cotton naked and steaming beneath. The contours of her thick body were as soft as pillows when Rochelle touched them. Cotton took Rochelle's hand and shoved it between her legs. She was shaved clean. Rochelle found her clit above her wet slit easily.

She felt Cotton's hand between her legs as well, tickling her clit with two fingers. Cotton moved down some and kissed Rochelle's neck, sending shockwaves throughout her body.

"Let me eat your pussy, Rochelle," Cotton begged. "Let me lick it. Please, baby. Let me."

"No . . ." Rochelle responded, but she couldn't find the energy to pull Cotton's hand away from her pussy. "We need to stop."

Cotton didn't want to hear that. She rolled her upper torso on top of Rochelle and held her still while kissing her passionately. Her fingers yanked at Rochelle's panties to get them out of her way. Then they were plunging in and out of Rochelle, pulling her pussy lips apart.

Rochelle loved the invasion. She didn't want Cotton to stop, but she had to. She didn't like girls, and . . .

Rochelle pushed Cotton off and hurried up from the bed. "Cotton . . ." She stood at the edge of the bed unable to move away.

Cotton stood up. Her beautiful body strode toward Rochelle. Rochelle watched her pendulous breasts sway as she neared, and the urge to suckle her light brown nipples overwhelmed her. She didn't know why she didn't want to sleep with Cotton. She'd done it before, and it was good. But for some reason, she couldn't bring herself to do it again.

Cotton pushed Rochelle into the wall and pressed her lips against hers again. Her hand dipped beneath Rochelle's nightshirt and found her wet pussy. "Stop resisting me, Rochelle," she managed to say. "Let it happen."

Rochelle pried herself out of Cotton's grip and ran to her bedroom, slamming the door behind her. Cotton went after her. But when she tried the handle, she found it locked. Rochelle sat on the edge of her bed, feeling horny and unsatisfied. She lay back on the bed as Cotton whispered, "Open the door, Rochelle. I don't want to wake up Lacy. Come on, baby."

Rochelle scooted on the bed and spread her legs. She was so turned on. Her own hands dipped between her legs and fondled her clit. When she closed her eyes, all she saw was Cotton kneeling between her thighs, licking her pussy. She sat up and looked around the room in frustration. "I need a fucking man."

Her eyes landed on a wadded up piece of paper sitting on the nightstand. She hurried to it and found it to be the phone number of the guy she'd met at the donut shop the other day. Marco.

Cotton drummed her nails on Rochelle's door. "Rochelle. Don't shut me out, Rochelle. I need you. Open the door. Please."

Rochelle picked up her phone and sent a text to his number: *hey. marco. this is rochelle. we met at my job. i was wondering if u wanted to hang out?*

TEN

I T WAS TEN A.M. WHEN LACY AWAKENED to scratching outside her bedroom window. She opened her eyes and saw Bunny lifting up the window from the outside. Seconds later, Bunny climbed through quietly, as she had been doing since she was twelve years old.

This morning Bunny wore tight black jeans and a thin leather jacket. She shed the jacket and pulled her arms into an orange, long-sleeved shirt with AUBURN stamped in blue letters on the front. Lacy never climbed out of bed. She lay there, staring at her friend. Bunny sat on a beanbag chair in the corner and tried unsuccessfully to shield the side of her face from Lacy.

Lacy asked, "Becky hit you again? Last night? After you got home."

Bunny's eyes focused on the floor. "Worse."

It wasn't the first time Bunny had arrived with a black eye, busted lip, or bleeding from the crotch. She had known abuse for many more years than it had been a stranger. Most of the time, Bunny didn't explain or talk about what happened. Lacy knew what happened. Talking about it made the situation worse. Bunny usually went about her day as if she were not hurt. And in a way, Lacy knew that Bunny had found a place to store away her pain long ago. Someplace that she revealed to no one. Yet Lacy asked, "What could be worse than getting your ass kicked?"

Bunny bit a corner of her lip. "Once she got to the the police station I explained that we'd been at some guy's house that got raided. She searched my room as soon as we got back home, thinking she would find some dope in there."

Lacy sat up then, suddenly alarmed. "She didn't . . ."

Tears sprang from Bunny's eyes. "She found my stash."

"How much, Bunny?"

"All of it. Sixteen thousand."

Lacy fell back onto the bed. "Fuck! And she took it all?"

"Every penny. Her and Rudy were out all night. They came home a little while ago with their eyes bugged out. My mom fell asleep on the couch. Rudy came into my bedroom. He had his dick in his hand. I ran out of the house so that I wouldn't kill him."

Lacy watched Bunny, not knowing what to say. "I know it took all you had not to spazz the fuck out. I told you to find another stash spot!"

Bunny stared back at Lacy, but she didn't say anything. Finally, she reached into her jacket pocket and pulled out one of the chrome nine-millimeters they had taken from Fat Freddy's. She held it loosely in her hand while staring at Lacy, tears spewing from her eyes. "You have no idea what I thought about doing to them. No idea."

Lacy looked at the gun, then into Bunny's eyes. "Were you going to kill them?"

Bunny swallowed hard. "Myself." Her tears flowed in torrential rains destined to flood flatlands and wash away her pain, as well as her hope for a better future.

Lacy got up and hurried to Bunny. The pistol thudded on the floor when Bunny let it go to embrace Lacy. Lacy slumped to the floor and embraced her best friend. It was all that she could do.

"Bunny, I'm sorry that happened to you. You don't deserve that."

Bunny did her best to speak through her tears. "That was all the money that I had in the world. What are we going to do now? I knew we should have found our own place months ago."

They had been saving for a year. Since the day Bunny climbed into Lacy's window, hopped in her bed, and confessed that she didn't like the way Rudy, her mother's new boyfriend, was looking at her. Lacy had listened, but she didn't tell Bunny she was imagining things, or that it would be okay this time. Although Bunny was young, she knew when a man was looking at her inappropriately. She'd been through it all before. And as Lacy held her that morning, she recalled a day some years before when Bunny told her that her stepfather, Patrick, had been raping her since she was old enough to remember. She'd told her mother, but Becky accused her of lying, and said that if Patrick had slept with her, it was only because Bunny had enticed him. She threatened to throw Bunny out of the house if she told anyone. Becky explained that Patrick paid the bills, and in her eyes, he was worth much more to Becky than Bunny.

Lacy had held her in the same way, telling Bunny that everything would be okay back then, even though she didn't believe it herself. Fast forward a few years. Patrick was serving twenty years in prison for raping some other young girl in a crack house, and now it was Rudy who was making eyes at Bunny while supplying the only paycheck in the house. It was all too familiar. Like a merry-go-round where the same fucked up bullshit happened to the same innocent girl over and over again.

"What are we going to do?" Bunny asked her once she had settled down. "That money was my only chance to get away and start a new life."

Lacy let her go and went back to sit on the edge of her bed. It was ten in the morning, but she was still sleepy. She wanted to ask Bunny to take a nap with her, but she knew Bunny wouldn't sleep after losing so much money. At the same time she didn't understand why Bunny still lived with her dope fiend mother. "I don't know," she answered. "I still have my money. Somewhere around thirteen thousand."

"We can't buy two cars and get an apartment with that."

"We can, but they'll be cheap cars."

"Fuck that," Bunny said. "I'll be damned if I'mma drive a Toyota when I'm out here doing all this bullshit. Besides, you need your money for college."

Lacy shook her head. "I told you. I'm not going to college. That's Rochelle's dream. Not mine."

Lacy and Bunny had already tried to rent an apartment, but no complex would rent to them without proof of income. That meant they had to prove that they were working and earning enough money to pay their rent on time. Cash wasn't enough. They could have bought a car or two, but then Rochelle would want to know where they'd gotten the money without a job. Lacy was a grown woman, but she wasn't sure that she was ready to answer that question. On top of that, she'd have to tell Rochelle that she didn't plan on ever going to school. Those were too many confessions for her to make at one time. She yearned to take the coward's way out. Get her apartment. Get her car. And talk to her sister in the aftermath. Once she was out on her own, Rochelle's scrutiny would no longer hinder her. Seemed like a great plan. But it wasn't working out.

Bunny let out an exasperated sigh. "You're stupid. I wish I had somebody that cared enough to help me go to school. My mama ain't never did shit for me. At least you know Rochelle cares. All she wants is to make sure you're okay."

"I don't have to go to school to do okay. I've never made anything below an A."

"That's why it makes so much sense for you to go to school. I don't know why you didn't apply for a scholarship. You would've gotten it."

Lacy stood and snatched a pair of jeans from the floor. "Fuck that. I don't want to live in no stuffy ass dorm with some ol' stuffy ass bitches that think they're better than me because their mommy and daddy got a little money. I want to make my own money. And that's what we're going to do."

Bunny stared at her. "Whatever. I'm tired of talking about this shit. Do what the fuck you want to do."

"I am." Lacy pulled on the jeans, then took off her night shirt.

Just then, she heard a voice in the hallway. She looked to Bunny and put a stiff index finger to her lips. Lacy crept to her door and cracked it open. She felt Bunny pressed against her body behind her. Together they saw Rochelle run down the hall toward them and lock herself in her bedroom. Cotton followed, running in the nude. She stopped at Rochelle's door and whispered, "Open the door, Rochelle. I don't want to wake up Lacy. Come on, baby."

Lacy's eyes bulged out of their sockets as she watched Cotton's hand dip between her legs and fondle herself outside of Rochelle's door. "Rochelle," Cotton panted. "Don't shut me out, Rochelle. I need you. Open the door. Please." Her hand moved frantically between her legs.

Lacy closed the door and sat down on the edge of the bed. She reached over and plucked a half-smoked blunt from an ashtray on the floor. She lit it as Bunny sat across from her on the beanbag. All of their previous discussions took a back seat to what they had just witnessed.

Bunny asked, "Are they still fucking?"

Lacy took a long hit and squinted as she blew out the smoke. "I don't know, man. But I wish Rochelle would decide if she's a lesbian or not. Cotton is crazy about her." She handed the blunt to Bunny. "Every time they're together, Cotton is all over her. Something has to give."

Bunny took a long hit on the blunt and held it in. She blew out a stream of smoke, then sucked in another.

Lacy reached for the blunt. "Puff, puff, pass, bitch. This shit ain't free."

Bunny asked, "Would it bother you—if she was gay?"

Lacy paused with the blunt poised in front of her lips. "I don't give a fuck. If she is, she is. Cotton is fine as hell. I wouldn't fuck her, but why should it bother me? She can do what she wants. I just think Rochelle should figure out what she wants. It obvious that she has feelings for Cotton too. She's scared though. If I had feelings like that, I wouldn't be scared of them. I'd just give into it. Fuck it." Lacy side-eyed Bunny. "Have you ever thought about eating pussy?" She hit the blunt while waiting on a response.

Bunny recoiled. "Me? No." She averted her eyes.

Lacy smiled as she blew smoke out of her nostrils. "Yes, you have. You're lying."

"I like dick too much."

Lacy passed the blunt to Bunny. "You wouldn't eat my pussy?"

Bunny held the blunt still. "What?"

Lacy giggled. "That's not a no."

"What are you asking me?"

"I'm asking if you would eat my pussy."

"I don't know," Bunny admitted. "I've thought about it." She hit the blunt with her eyes locked on Lacy's. "Maybe I've thought about it too much. I like men. You're pretty and all, but I don't want a woman." She handed the blunt back to Lacy. It was now a roach that she had to pinch with her fingernails. "Would you eat my pussy?"

A smile spread across Lacy's lips. "It depends. I'd have to want a nut real bad. And that motherfucker better smell like Summer's Eve."

They both cracked up laughing. Sex wasn't something they spoke about often. It didn't matter that they were friends. Lacy was relieved that she could talk so openly with Bunny. To be honest, she would sleep with Bunny. She loved Bunny as more than a sister. She was the one person she would do anything for. If Bunny wanted to have a sexual relationship, she would do it. They couldn't be exclusive, but Lacy would do it. That's how close they were—but not close enough to actually try it.

Bunny sat deep into the beanbag chair and stared off into space. "I can't believe my mama stole all my money."

"Don't worry. I got you. I'll give you a couple thousand. We'll get more . . . somehow."

"What about those dudes we met last night?"

"Rich and Dame?"

"The cops didn't find their stash. Isn't that what you said? He had money and dope?"

Lacy nodded and stubbed out the blunt duck. "Mm-hm. He had hella bread and dope. I don't know how they didn't find it."

Bunny nodded. "Dame is in the hospital. He had a shootout with the cops, so he won't be home anytime soon."

"What about Rich? He might be there."

Bunny stood and paced a little. "I don't know. The cops might not have let him go. Especially if they think he's hustling with Dame. The house has got to be in Rich's name. He's the oldest."

Lacy leaned back on her bed. "It's worth taking a look into. Maybe we can get your money back tonight."

Bunny smiled. "Okay."

Lacy licked her lips while spreading her legs. She took two fingers and squeezed her vagina lips together. "Now come on over here and eat my pussy."

Bunny threw the beanbag chair at Lacy. "Eat that, bitch!"

ELEVEN

ROCHELLE STEPPED OUT OF THE SHOWER feeling like a brand new woman. She toweled off, then pulled on a pair of black lace panties and a matching bra. She stood, looking into the mirror as she teased her natural hair while deciding what to do with it when Cotton walked into the bathroom.

Rochelle met her eyes through the reflection. "Don't you know how to knock?"

Cotton wore her sheer robe, black thongs, no bra, and a grimace. She leaned with her back against the counter and held a smoking blunt in her hand. "I haven't been knocking. Why should I start now?"

Rochelle rolled her eyes.

Cotton's gaze tiptoed over Rochelle's body. Rochelle wasn't as thick as Cotton, but she had a nice figure all the same. Round breasts, a plump ass, and a tight stomach. Cotton hit the blunt. "Are you going to the club with that on?"

"I'm not going to the club. If I do, it'll be later."

"Where are you going?"

Rochelle glanced at her. "To mind my business and leave yours alone."

"Is that how we talk to each other now?"

"I'm going out on a date, if you must know."

"A date? With who?"

Rochelle tried to shrug off the question as if it didn't affect her, but she couldn't hide the fact that it did. "I met a guy at the donut shop. He's taking me out to eat. If I don't have a good time, I'll show up at the club. If I do like him, we'll go someplace else."

Cotton hit the blunt again and side-eyed her. "Roscoe won't like that. Yesterday you were late. Today you're not going in . . ."

"Fuck Roscoe." She dabbed some Pink Oil onto her palm and massaged it into her hair. "I'm tired of his sleazy ass anyway."

Cotton sucked her teeth. "You ain't tired of that pay check though."

Rochelle dropped her arms and stared at Cotton. "What do you want?"

Cotton dropped the blunt into an ashtray on the sink. "To stay twenty-eight forever, ten million dollars, a brand new Ferrari, and to make you scream my name every day for the rest of your life."

Rochelle let out a long sigh. "Do you ever stop?"

Cotton shook her head. "Not when it comes to you."

"Cotton . . ."

Cotton eased in close to Rochelle and allowed her sheer robe to fall open. Her fat titties brushed Rochelle's arm. "I know you want me, Rochelle. You need to stop playing."

Rochelle nudged her away. "Ain't nobody playing with you, Cotton."

Cotton's lips touched Rochelle's ear. "I'll bet that pussy is as wet as mine right now. Isn't it?" She reached down and rubbed her hand up and down Rochelle's ass cheek. "Let me find out."

Rochelle turned to face her. "I don't want to get anything started with you, Cotton. I love you, but not like that."

"I don't believe you." Cotton kissed her ear. Instead of pulling away, Rochelle leaned into it. "See. Look at that." Cotton's tongue snaked out and ran a circle around Rochelle's earlobe. Rochelle moaned. "Listen at you. I know what you want." Cotton's hand sank lower until her fingers were wedged between Rochelle's legs and she was fingering her from behind. "I knew that pussy was wet for me. I want to eat you so bad that I can taste it." Her fingers pulled out and rubbed circles around Rochelle's clit while her tongue swirled circles in Rochelle's ear.

Rochelle gripped the edge of the sink and squeezed until her knuckles were white and she couldn't squeeze any more. "Cotton. Please stop. Please."

Cotton's fingers worked harder, slamming in and out of Rochelle's pussy. Cotton leaned over and kissed Rochelle on the mouth. When Rochelle pulled away, Cotton's lips gave chase until they caught up and she forced Rochelle to kiss her. But just as Rochelle seemed to give in, she jerked away from Cotton and retreated to the far wall of the bathroom and stood there panting.

"I don't want you like that, Cotton."

Cotton wiped the spots on her lips where they were still warm from Rochelle's. "How are you going to turn me away? I killed a nigga for us . . ."

"You can't hold that over my head," Rochelle spat. "It's all a part of the game."

"Game. Is that what I am to you? A fucking game?"

"You're my best friend and my sister, Cotton. That's what you are. Leave it at that."

They were still staring each other down when Lacy and Bunny appeared in the bathroom doorway. Lacy asked, "Am I interrupting something?"

Cotton's eyes never left Rochelle's. "Hmph. I was on my way out." She pushed past Bunny and Lacy.

Bunny squeezed into a corner of the bathroom. "What's wrong with her?"

Rochelle moved back to the mirror and picked up an afro pick. "She'll be alright."

Lacy slid in next to Rochelle. She looked her older sister up and down. "What are you getting all dressed up for?"

"Who says I'm getting dressed up?"

"You're wearing panties without holes in them for one."

"And they match your bra," Bunny added.

Rochelle rolled her eyes. "Is it that obvious?"

Lacy shrugged. "You never go out. Last time you had a date was with that guy Jose. The Mexican."

"He was Puerto Rican. Not Mexican. There's a difference."

Lacy smirked. "They both eat enchiladas. But that was over a year ago. Who's this guy?"

"I met him at the donut shop. He was tall and handsome. Nice clothes. Nice car. Helluva talk game. I figured I'd give him a try."

Lacy nodded along. "Since he's picking you up, can me and Bunny borrow your car tonight? We want to go out."

"Who said *he* was picking me up?"

"That's what guys do on a date, isn't it?" Bunny asked.

"You should try *dating* men instead of jumping in the bed as soon as you meet them. Your fast ass may actually like being treated like a lady." Rochelle smoothed out a thin, blue silk scarf and wrapped it around the crown of her head. "Besides, I don't know what most girls do, but I drive myself to the first date. I don't know this man. If he's crazy, a jackass, or a rapist, I want a way out. Can't run in somebody else's car." She noted the way Lacy and Bunny's faces drooped. "I can give y'all a ride someplace if you need it."

Lacy shook her head. "Nah. It's okay. We'll find a way."

Rochelle watched the girls walk out, wondering what mischief they had in mind. Lacy was smart. Too smart for her own good. Rochelle wanted to tell her not to go out, but Lacy was nineteen. She could do what she wanted to do. That's what worried Rochelle the most, letting go. Maybe she'd spoiled her too much. Rochelle had always been careful with Lacy, because she didn't know how their mother's death affected her. Maybe she held on too tight and realized it too late. Lacy would have to make her own mistakes in life. That was the only way she would learn.

Thirty minutes later, Rochelle stepped out of the house in tight black leggings, heels, and a blue blouse to match her scarf. It was eight-fifteen when she climbed into her sedan and prepared to leave. Cotton would be leaving in an hour to go to the club. She unconsciously peeked at Cotton's bedroom window and saw an opening in the blinds. Cotton was spying on her. Rochelle started her car and pulled out of the driveway, determined to get her life back in order.

She pulled into the Baby Doe's parking lot at eight-forty-five. It was a Thursday night, a week before Christmas, on the heels of the coronavirus pandemic. Not many people were out. Rochelle pulled on her facemask before getting out of the car.

She spotted Marco seated in the back of the restaurant as soon as she walked in. A hostess led her to his table. He was dressed in a navy blue suit with a white T-shirt and clean Air Force One's. He wore a blue facemask that matched his outfit and gave her a short hug when she got to his table. He pulled out her chair, and once she was seated, he handed her a single yellow rose. She smiled so hard that her cheeks hurt. It had been a long time since a man had given her a rose.

"This place is nice," she commented, looking around.

Marco sat across from her. "You've never been here?"

"I didn't know it existed."

"Not many people come here. I love it."

Rochelle leaned over the table a bit. "I think we're far enough apart to take off our masks. I need to remember what you look like." Marco chuckled as he pulled down his mask. Rochelle stared at his chiseled face and thought that he looked so much more handsome than she remembered. Plus he was in real clothes, not like the rags worn by most of the other men that's tried to talk to her. "There you are," she declared.

"You like what you see?"

She nodded. "I do. I like it."

"Now you."

Rochelle unhooked her mask from one ear and pulled it off. She appreciated the smile that spread across Marco's face when he saw her. She couldn't breathe under his scrutiny. "Do you like me?" She managed to ask.

"Much more than you know." They smiled at each other for a moment. Then Marco said, "I took a chance and ordered for you. Everyone likes chicken, so I got you a baked chicken breast, peas, and rice. Is that okay?"

"Outstanding choice."

"Good. When the waitress comes back, you can tell her what you want to drink."

Rochelle picked up a drink menu and surveyed it. "Marco, there are no prices on here."

He smiled. "If you have to ask the price in a place like this, you can't afford it."

She put down the menu. "It's obvious that you make a lot of money. What do you do?"

He drummed his fingers on the surface of the table. "I'm going to tell you this one time. No more. If you ask me a question, make sure that you can handle the answer. You have an idea about who I am and what I do already. Do you really need me to tell you?"

"I don't have a clue what you do."

"What do you think I do?"

She slumped in her seat a bit. "Something illegal."

"I make enough money to feed you in this nice restaurant where we're the only black faces. What else do you need to know?"

"If you don't want to tell me, you just have to say so. I have two jobs. I work at the donut shop in the mornings, and I bartend in a strip club at night. My roommate is a stripper. My sister doesn't do anything but eat up my food. I pay my bills on time. And I haven't been on a date in so long that I can't recall how the last one went. I don't have anything to hide. Why can't you be the same? I don't care if you sell drugs. I don't care if you rob people. I just want you to be real. If you lie to me now, you'll lie to me later, and I'll have to cut you. You might as well tell me the truth from the get go and let me deal with it so there will be no surprises in case I decide to make you my man."

Marco stared at her for a long time. "You want me to be your man?"

"I said if I decide. You're cute. You're smart. You make a lot of money. And you like me. I want to know more about you, but I'm considering it but it's too early to tell. You might poot in your sleep, I don't know."

He smiled. Then he chuckled. Then he threw his head back and laughed. When he was done, he looked her in the eye. "I won't ever lie to you. If I don't want you to know something, I just won't tell you. I don't have to lie to you."

"Okay," she said, wanting to test him. "Do you sell drugs?"

"Sometimes. I work too. I manage a cellphone repair shop. It's nothing big, but I make more money than a lot of people. It's enough to get by."

"Do you own a house or rent an apartment?"

"Own a house."

"Kids?"

He shook his head no. "A blessing and a curse. You?"

"I raised my little sister, Lacy. She was enough. Maybe in a couple of years."

He nodded. "You know what you want out of life, huh?"

"I don't know how to get it. That's my problem."

He was gorgeous. She had to squeeze her thighs together every time she looked at him. She was so hard up that she was trying to find a way to tell him that she didn't want to eat in some fancy restaurant. She wanted him to take her back to the house he owned and fuck the shit out of her. She needed to feel the punishment of a big strong man abusing her body to get the thoughts of Cotton's softness out of her mind. She opened her lips to tell him—*Take me home. We don't have to love each other. Just love me for the night, and I'll be happy*—but his phone rang, interrupting her.

He looked at the Caller ID. "I've got to get this." Into the phone, he said, "Yeah. It's me. No. Are you fucking serious? Now." He casted a glance to Rochelle. "I'm busy. I can't just up and leave. I'm with somebody. Okay. No. Alright. *Alright!* Goddamn it. I'm on the way." When he hung up, he grimaced to tell her, "Look, I know we were having a good time, but I have to go."

She sat back in her chair. "Are you kidding me?"

He shook his head. "Something important came up. You can stay if you want to. I'll leave my credit card. Eat what you want. My treat. Maybe we can do this again some other time."

Rochelle stood up. "I wouldn't dare."

Marco stood up just as she was storming out of the restaurant. "Rochelle!"

But she was gone.

TWELVE

ROCHELLE ALMOST DIDN'T SHOW UP FOR WORK. She didn't fear losing her job. That was the least of her worries. She could handle Roscoe. All she had to do was flirt with him if he acted like he was mad. Men like Roscoe were weak creatures who reacted more to the possibility of getting some pussy than *actually* getting some.

Rochelle feared a confrontation with Cotton. They'd separated on bad terms and her showing up at work proved that Cotton was right. A man would only let Rochelle down. She couldn't win against such an argument, especially when Marco ending their date early demonstrated the truth in Cotton's statement.

She drove around Atlanta for a little while as she debated going to work. Finally, after much contemplation, she decided to face the music. Her only alternative was to sit at home and watch Netflix. She'd much rather make tips. Money always made her feel better.

She arrived at Queen of Spades a little after midnight. Thursdays were always popping at Queen's, even during the pandemic. She found Juicy behind the bar, struggling to fill orders . . . again. Rochelle walked back, put down her bag, and grabbed a handful of tickets to help Juicy. Neither spoke to the other, though Rochelle could feel the heat of Juicy's anger at Rochelle being late. She thought she heard Juicy smack her lips, but Juicy's facemask got in the way. Rochelle smiled to herself, thinking that Juicy was lucky she showed up at all.

She spotted Cotton giving a lap dance on the other side of the club. She wore a gold thong and bra set that made her sparkle when the other girls seemed so dull. Cotton looked up and kept her eyes on Rochelle as she turned around and wiggled her ass in the customer's face. Through her sheer gold facemask, Cotton's mouth crept open. Her tongue snaked out and licked her lips. She twerked on the guy's lap, but Rochelle knew the show was meant for her. She turned away and finished filling drink orders.

Cotton sat at the bar right across from Rochelle a few minutes later. "What happened to your date?"

Rochelle refused to look at her. "I didn't feel like staying."

Cotton laughed. "You never could lie to me." She leaned over the bar and lifted Rochelle's chin with a curled finger. "I'm not going to say 'I told you so,' even though I should. I wanted you to have a good time. Don't think I'm over here praying for you to be unhappy. I'm not. I love you, Rochelle. That won't change today, tomorrow, or the day after that. I will always love you . . . even if you don't love me back."

Rochelle turned away to mask the tears in her eyes. "Cotton, don't do this here."

Cotton sat back down. "I'm sorry it didn't go well for you. Men are born disappointments. Can't kiss. Can't fuck. Can't support a family. What are they good for?"

Rochelle's eyes trained on a scratch in the bar's surface. "He got a phone call and had to leave. It wasn't his fault."

Cotton thought about that. "Did you like him?"

She looked to Cotton. "I still do."

"Even after he left you?"

She nodded. "Yeah. I hardly know him, but I think I could like him a lot."

Cotton sucked her teeth and turned in her chair to face the club. She didn't say anything more.

Rochelle stared at her. "I thought you wanted me to be happy."

"I do." Cotton stood up. She leaned over the bar and pulled down her facemask to kiss Rochelle on the cheek, causing Juicy to gasp. When Rochelle pulled away, Cotton said, "I want you to be happy *with me*. No one else."

Rochelle wanted to protest. Cotton had never acted so boldly in public, but something caught her eye behind Cotton. She looked deeper into the club, into the VIP section and saw the face of a man that she never thought she would see again—a face she never wanted to see again.

MARCO'S PHONE RANG as soon as he walked into the club. He spotted Genesis way in the back, seated in a perch that he assumed was the VIP section. What section would Genesis sit in besides the VIP? He paused to look at his phone. It was Blake. He didn't answer. Two seconds later, Blake texted him: *call me now*

"Shit," Marco muttered to himself as he headed toward a sign reading RESTROOM. The restroom looked vacant. He hurried past the stalls and pushed them open, making the doors bang against the walls. Once he was satisfied that he was alone, he called Blake. "This better be good. You have no idea what you're interrupting."

"It is," Blake replied. "Devon Wright was the point man while Genesis was serving time. He handled all of his affairs until Genesis was released."

Marco exhaled his frustration. "Tell me something I don't know. I've been with these guys. I know all of that."

"Did you know that Devon Wright had significant land holdings in North Carolina and Pennsylvania? Millions of dollars tied up in real estate. And get this. He didn't buy any of that until your boy Genesis was locked up—years after he was locked up."

"So you think Devon was stealing from him?"

"I know he was."

Marco nodded. "Then it's likely that Genesis knew it too and had him hit."

"That means watch your ass."

"You didn't have to call to tell me that." It all made sense. He had already surmised why Devon's house was bigger than Genesis' townhouse. It was easy to piece together. The only thing that puzzled Marco, was why Devon hadn't killed Genesis first? "In the future," Marco told Blake. "Don't call me. I'll call you." He hung up and headed out into the club.

COTTON FOLLOWED ROCHELLE'S GAZE and saw what spooked her friend. She spotted a handsome, dark-skinned man with a slick bald head and salt and pepper goatee. He didn't dress like the young men who came in wearing skinny jeans and colorful shirts. He wore all black. Baggy slacks. A black silk shirt. Nice shoes too. Cotton glanced at his wrists and neck. He wore no jewelry, yet that fact only added to her curiosity, because he appeared rich and powerful.

Cotton looked to Rochelle, who was still staring at the man. "Rochelle, who is that?"

Rochelle wiped her hands on a towel. "I gotta get out of here." She picked up her bag.

Juicy saw her about to leave and protested, "Where you going? You just got here."

Rochelle paid her no attention.

Cotton met her at the entrance to the back of the bar. "Wait a second. Tell me what's going on."

"Get out of my way, Cotton."

"Not until you tell me what's going on."

"Who is that guy up there?"

Rochelle met her eyes. "He's the man that killed my mama."

MARCO STEPPED UP TO THE VIP where Genesis was seated with Juan and Jason, two of his closest workers. He'd met them before.

"My man, Mondo!" Genesis called out as Marco slid onto the bench seat next to him. "Sorry I had to pull you away from what you were doing, but we need to talk." He looked to Juan. "Give me a minute."

Juan and Jason called two dancers over and slid to the edge of the bench to give Marco and Genesis the privacy they needed to talk.

When they were gone, Genesis turned back to Marco. "What were you doing when I called?"

Marco almost laughed. "I was on a date."

"For real?"

"Yeah. I met this little chick the other day. We were eating dinner. I hadn't been there ten minutes when you called."

Genesis smiled. "She let you leave?"

"She didn't have a choice."

"You like her?"

"Yeah. But money comes first. It sounded urgent on the phone, so I came. Maybe she'll understand. Maybe she won't."

Genesis watched Marco with curious eyes. "Most niggas wouldn't have traded a piece of pussy for money." His smile faded. "When you leave here, call her. Promise to take her out again. I'll pay for it."

"You ain't gotta do all that."

"That's why I like you," Genesis said. "You're all business. No bullshit."

"Is there any other way to live?"

Genesis' smile crinkled to a tight grimace. "I got some bad news today. You hear about Devon?"

Marco shook his head and hoped his face didn't betray his lie. "Nah. Where's he at?"

"In a morgue. Somebody peeled his wig back. Ran up in his crib and did him dirty. Took all his money. Shit was nasty."

Marco tried his best to look surprised. "I heard about a murder out in Buckhead, but I had no idea it was him. You know who did it?"

Genesis shrugged. "Niggas making money got a lot of enemies. A motherfucker's own mama ain't a friend when you getting money. Either she'll tell on you or spend your dough when you're locked up. I've been there. You can never be too careful. Devon got careless, so it cost him his life. It won't happen to me."

"How can you be so sure?"

Genesis made sure to look dead into Marco's eyes. "Because I don't trust nobody. I'll do business with you. I'll kick it with you. But I don't trust you. No one. Which brings me to my point in meeting with you tonight." Genesis let his eyes wander to one of the dancers with Juan and Jason. He watched her ass bounce for a moment then turned back to Marco. "Since Devon's dumbass fucked up and got caught slipping, I need someone to take over the product he was selling. I don't know who his clientele was—don't want to know—so you'll have to find your own, but I need someone to take what he was moving so there are no rifts in cash flow. Do you think you can handle that?"

Marco's heart beat wildly in his chest. This was the moment he'd been working toward his entire career. He took deep breaths to mask his excitement. "Yeah. I think I can do that. It might take a minute on the first run, but after that, I should be straight."

"Good. I'll have Jason fill you in on the details a little later. He may give you some names of dudes Devon served." Genesis eased back in his seat and looked to the dancers again. "And since I ruined your date, let's get some of these girls over here to celebrate your new opportunity."

Marco smiled and shook Genesis' hand when it was offered to him. He hated the way drug dealers talked and acted like businessmen, as if they weren't selling poison to their communities. He wanted to arrest Genesis, even though he knew prison was too good for him. Men like Genesis deserved to die. Not because they broke the law. Fuck the law. He needed to die because he didn't care about anyone but himself, and he was willing to let others die around him so that he could thrive. He didn't give a damn that Devon was dead as long as he had another hustler to fill his shoes. In Marco's eyes, Genesis was the worst kind of human being on the face of the earth.

COTTON COULDN'T BELIEVE HER EARS. "He killed your mother?" She sat Rochelle down on a stool beside the bar. Rochelle casted side glances toward the VIP section, but the look of fear didn't dwell in her eyes as it had before. "I thought your mama was at work when she died."

Rochelle nodded. "She was. My mama worked as a gas station attendant. Her boyfriend, Michael, owned the place. Michael sold a little dope on the side, but he wasn't any good at it. A bigger dealer fronted him some coke, and he fucked the money up. When the dealer came to collect, he killed Michael. My mama was working when it happened."

Cotton dropped her gaze. "And it was him . . . up there. He killed her too?"

Rochelle stood up. "That's why I have to leave. I can't stand to be here."

Cotton stood to stop her. "He doesn't know who you are. He can't hurt you."

"He might remember me. I was at his trial, but I'm not worried about him hurting me."

Cotton glanced down and noticed Rochelle's hand stuffed into her bag. She didn't have to wonder what she was gripping beneath the shield of leather. "You don't have to hurt him here, Rochelle. There's another way."

MARCO WAS INTO HIS THIRD DRINK when the sexiest redbone he'd ever seen walked into the VIP section. She was short with thick thighs and soft breasts. Her blonde afro was perfectly round and teased. He'd been watching dancers for an hour, and not one had struck him the way she did. The only problem was that she wasn't walking to him.

The girl kept her eyes on Genesis the whole time that she navigated past Juan and Jason tossing dollar bills at dancers twerking while on all fours on the floor. She leaned over Genesis with her hands planted on the back of the bench where he sat. Even from where he sat beside Genesis, her perfume made Marco's head swoon. "You want a dance, sweetie?" He heard her ask Genesis.

Genesis reached out and rubbed her ass. "Thank you, but no. Not from you."

The beauty frowned. "You don't want a dance? There isn't another girl in here that can do what I can."

Genesis smiled and pushed her back. "I'm sure you're good at what you do. But what about her?" He pointed to the bar at the front of the club. "I saw you talking to her earlier. Bring her to me."

Marco followed Genesis' pointing finger, but he didn't see the woman in question.

The dancer with the blonde afro did. She looked toward the bar in horror. "She's not a dancer, sweetie. She ain't nothing but a bartender. Let me take care of you."

"That's why I want her. She ain't a ho like you." Genesis snapped. "Go get her and get the fuck out of my face."

Marco chuckled to himself because he knew that's what Genesis expected him to do. The girl walked to the bar. Marco still could not see who the stripper was talking to.

"I don't fuck with strippers," Genesis told him. "Especially the ones who think they're the prettiest bitches on the planet. I like a regular chick. A bitch with bucked teeth and stretch marks and shit. A hood bitch that can fuck for days and won't complain when she doesn't see me for a week."

Marco listened as the blonde stripper walked back toward them with another girl in tow. His eyes opened wide when he saw who it was. Rochelle locked eyes with him as she climbed the VIP stairs, but if she was shocked to see him, she didn't let on.

When the girls reached them. The blonde one said, "Here she is."

Genesis stood up and looked Rochelle over. "Hey, baby. How are you doing?"

"Good," she said.

"My name is Genesis. This is my man, Mondo."

Rochelle casted a glance to Marco. "Mon-do?"

Marco nodded, hoping she didn't make a scene. "*Mondo*. And you are . . ."

Rochelle snarled to say, "Nina."

Marco raised his eyebrows. "Nina?"

She nodded. "Nina." Then Rochelle turned to Genesis. "My girl Cotton said you wanted to talk to me."

Genesis took her by the hand and led her away from the VIP. "Yeah. I saw you down by the bar and . . ."

Marco watched them walk to a table in a corner of the club. They sat. Cotton watched them to. Then she looked down on Marco, and shrugged. "You want a dance?"

Marco shook his head. "Nah."

Cotton didn't get up to look for another customer. She remained on the bench next to him. "I don't feel like dancing anyway."

Together they stared at Genesis and Rochelle talking, laughing, and looking like they were having a good time.

THIRTEEN

ALTHOUGH THEY HAD ONLY BEEN THERE ONCE, Lacy and Bunny had no problem finding the townhouse where Dame and Rich lived, after being dropped off by the Uber. They planned to call another car from the gas station once they finished.

The neighborhood was quiet, unsurprisingly. It was one in the morning. The lights were off in most homes. Lacy and Bunny walked close to the houses and made sure to keep in the shadows. Both tucked their faces in black facemasks. They also wore leather gloves. The only accessory Lacy wore that might stand out was her signature Green Grinch hat. She wore the hat because it was the last thing her mother had ever given her. In fact, she'd given one to Lacy and one to Rochelle on the same morning before she left for work. She never returned. For her the hat was sentimental. It also helped to mask her identity. A lot of people had security cameras mounted outside their homes, not to mention doorbell cameras. The mask and hat ensured her anonymity.

They made it to the house shortly after entering the neighborhood. They noticed that Rich's Chrysler 300 was not in the driveway. They paused on the side of a house across the street, watching for any sign of movement inside. Nothing. All of the lights were out. They huddled close together because it was cold out.

"You think he's in there asleep?" Lacy asked Bunny.

Bunny shivered. "I don't know. His car isn't here."

"The cops could have taken it for evidence."

"Can they do that?"

Lacy shrugged. "I don't know. I think so. For drugs . . . maybe."

Bunny sighed. "He could be inside."

Lacy reached into her waistband and pulled out the chrome nine millimeter that they'd taken from Fat Freddy. She pulled back the slide slowly, chambering a round. "He better pray he doesn't wake up if he is."

They crept toward the house and noticed no home security warning signs. Bunny went to the front door and found it locked. They walked around the back to a sliding glass door. Bunny placed her gloved palms on the glass and tried to slide it open. It budged an inch, but no farther. Lacy looked in the door's housing track and noticed a short wooden stick blocking its path. She found a thin nail file in her coat pocket and gave it to Bunny. Bunny jimmied the nail file between a gap in the two doors and lifted the stick out of the housing track. When she tried the door again, it slid open as smoothly as syrup sliding over the edge of a shortstack. Bunny pulled out her gun too as they stepped inside. Just in case.

The inside of the house was a mess. Though it was dark, they made out the couch cushions strewn about the floor. Large gashes in the pillows told the girls that the police had ripped into them with knives, no doubt looking for drugs. One couch was overturned. The kitchen was much the same. Food containers that were supposed to be refrigerated had been left out to spoil. The stench of sour milk invaded the thick mask, choking Lacy a bit. It was a disgusting situation, but the state of Rich and Dame's home told them that no one was there.

Both girls tucked their pistols back in their pants.

The carpeted stairs were plush and soft as they silently climbed. At the top, they paused to listen. All of the upstairs doors were closed, but they didn't hear a sound. After a moment of listening, Lacy gestured for them to keep moving. They continued down the hall until they reached the two adjacent bedrooms. Bunny and Lacy pulled out their pistols again. They didn't think anyone was home, but closed doors were something to take seriously. Bunny stood in the hallway while Lacy pushed Dame's bedroom door open, leading with her gun.

The blinds over the windows were drawn, emitting light from a streetlamp outside into the room. Lacy could see clearly. This room was a mess too. There were no covers on the bed. The mattress had been ripped open and its stuffing littered in clumps on the floor. The closet door stood wide open, its contents tossed about the floor as well.

Lacy hurried inside the closet and kicked away the clothes covering the corner where she'd found the drugs and money. She got down on all fours and pulled up the carpet. The floorboard was harder to pry up than she remembered, but she got it up all the same. The hole was empty. She thrust her hand inside and fished around. She felt rigid two-by-fours and a fluffy patch of insulation.

Lacy walked out into the hall, where Bunny stood with her eyes on the closed bedroom door across the hall. "It's not there," she whispered to Bunny.

Bunny's shoulders slumped when she heard the news. "What?"

"It's gone. Nothing is there. Rich must have taken it."

"Shit," Bunny muttered, then looked at the closed bedroom door. "Do you think he moved it? Maybe put it in his bedroom?"

"I don't know. I doubt it. I would have gotten the shit out of here altogether. If the cops came once, they'd probably come again. If he was smart, that's what he would have done."

Bunny kept looking at the closed door. "Fuck that. I didn't come all the way out here to go home empty handed. I'm going in there."

Lacy looked at the closed door and got a bad feeling. Something didn't feel right, but she didn't say anything. Bunny *needed* this money. It wasn't a *want* type of situation. If she didn't get paid, there was no telling what was going to happen when she went home. She lived in a bubble of uncertainty that threatened to pop every waking moment. Lacy had to help her in some way.

Bunny raised her pistol with one hand and gripped the door knob with the other. She pushed the door open and barely had time to back out of the way when the first shotgun blast exploded in the bedroom, blinding her. Luckily, she'd caught a glimpse of movement inside the room before he fired, and she was able to scoot out of the way. Once she was in the clear, another shot clapped in the night. The door behind her blew off its hinges and slammed into a far wall of Dame's bedroom.

"Come on in here, nigga!" Rich called out. "I heard you coming."

Lacy and Bunny exchanged looks. They were on the wrong side of the door. In order to get down the stairs, they'd have to run past the open doorway. They both gripped their pistols in tight fists. They had never been in this situation before. The prospect of one of them dying was very real for the first time.

A ratcheting sound clanked inside the room. Lacy thought he was reloading. The thought unnerved her, because she realized that they could have gotten out of there and failed to. Rich cocked the shotgun. Then silence.

Lacy crouched as low as she could. Bunny did the same, but behind her. Lacy eased to the open doorway and perched just on the side. It was dark in there, she thought. The shotgun blast effected his eyes. There was no way he would see her gun. She pointed it inside the room and let off a shot.

"Goddamn!" Rich shouted.

Lacy hopped up and ran past the doorway, blindly popping rounds inside the room, hoping to hit something. In the burst of lights, she thought that she saw Rich slumped on the floor bleeding within the split second that she had to look.

On the other side of the door, Lacy crouched and waited. She looked over at Bunny. Bunny mirrored her on the other side with her gun at the ready. After a second of silence, they heard the gentle sound of gurgling coming from inside the room. Gurgling and wheezing.

Lacy stood up by sliding her back against the wall. She reached her hand inside the room and felt around on the wall for a light switch. Once her fingers found it, she turned on the light and retreated back to the hall.

Nothing.

No sound.

No reaction.

Lacy risked a peek inside. Rich laid slumped on the bed, bleeding from a bullet wound in his stomach. His pistol-grip shotgun lay on the floor at his feet. Lacy rushed into the room and kicked the shotgun away. Bunny came in behind her. Rich looked up from the bed and smiled, blood staining his teeth.

Lacy knelt down beside Rich. "Where's the money?"

Instead of answering right away, Rich tried to sit up. "I knew it was you two bitches. I told Dame not to trust you." He looked up to Bunny. "I liked you. Fucked up what you're doing."

Lacy said, "Tell us where the money is, and we'll call an ambulance on the way out."

Rich finally sat up, clutching his belly. "You ain't calling no ambulance. Y'all gonna kill me. I know who you are."

"I'll call an . . ."

"Genesis is gonna find out who you are. It's only a matter of time."

Bunny asked, "Who the fuck is Genesis?"

"Don't play stupid, bitch. You know who the fuck Genesis is. You did the same thing to Devon. He'll find out who you are. You ain't got to worry about that . . ."

Bunny walked over and pressed the gun to his head. "Fuck you and fuck Genesis too. All I want is the money. Tell me where it is." She pulled back the hammer on the pistol. "Try me."

Rich looked up into her eyes. "I haven't hidden anything. It's right there on the dresser."

Bunny looked over and saw a shoebox on the dresser. She hurried there and knocked off the lid with the barrel of her pistol. Inside lay stacks of cash money. Hundreds, fifties, twenties. "Holy shit."

Lacy looked over to where Bunny stood and tried to peer into the box from a distance. As soon as they were distracted, Rich leapt up and knocked the pistol from Lacy's hand. Before she could react, he cocked back and punched Lacy in the eye, knocking her to the floor. Rich knelt to pick up Lacy's pistol but hesitated as he winced in pain from the hole in his abdomen.

Bunny dropped the box and unloaded on him, firing round after round until he slumped to the floor and rolled onto his back. Even when he lay motionless, Bunny stood over him yelling, "Die motherfucker, die!" She pulled the trigger until her gun was empty.

Bunny knelt next to Lacy. "You alright?"

Lacy sat up with a hand over her eye. "Hell, nah. That nigga knocked the fuck out of me." She moved her hand.

Bunny winced. "That shit is gonna be black in the morning."

"That bad?"

"Yeah."

Lacy climbed to her feet. "I'll buy a steak on the way home with this nigga's money." She kicked Rich's dead body before they took the money and left.

FOURTEEN

IT WAS BRICK COLD OUT, but Marco drove with his window down so that he could sober up. It had been a long night. Drink after drink after drink. It was nine a.m. and he hadn't slept a wink. The liquor hit him so hard because he wasn't a drinker, especially not while he was on the job. His sobriety guaranteed his safety. But last night . . . sitting and watching Rochelle flirt with Genesis unnerved him. Cotton, the dancer, offered to take him into the Champagne Room, but he didn't want a dance from her, or any other stripper. His mind had been focused on Rochelle and why she'd given the name Nina.

That's what he thought about as he drove toward the Colorful Confections Donut and Cupcake Shop. He had just pulled into the parking lot when his phone rang. It was Blake. He answered reluctantly.

"I'm not going to anymore murder scenes, Blake."

"I'm not asking you this time. This is really just a courtesy call to give you a heads up."

He drove past the Aldi's and had to slam on the brakes to avoid an old lady pushing a shopping cart. Her facemask had ridden up over her eyes, so she hadn't seen his car approaching. "Heads up on what?"

"Another murder."

"Are you fucking serious?" Some white guy helped the old lady out of the street, and Marco drove on. "What is this a serial thing?"

"Looks like it. The vics name was Richard Staton. The streets called him Rich. DEA had a file on him longer than a country mile. They just raided his place the other night. Had a shootout with his cousin, agents say they almost killed the little bastard too."

"Was Staton arrested?"

"Nah. His little cousin got caught with a quarter ki and a burner. He admitted that it was his. They didn't find anything else."

"Was he connected to Genesis?"

"We believe so. There's no hardcore evidence, but it's likely. Genesis doesn't move anything himself. He's insulated. With his boy Devon gone, he's missing a big piece in his distribution channels, but I'm sure Staton and Genesis crossed paths before. So yeah . . . I think this murder is connected to the others. I'm willing to bet my balls on it."

Marco spotted a burgundy car parked outside the donut shop. He pulled in next to it and spotted Rochelle inside the shop wearing her Grinch hat and a black facemask. He looked at the car again, then asked, "Any sightings of the getaway car?"

"I wish. I asked every neighbor, checked every surveillance camera within a ten-mile radius. Nobody saw a burgundy sedan. Everything else seems the same. This whole thing drives me bat shit. It's the same guys. I feel it in my bones."

Marco climbed out of his car and leaned on his door. He glanced inside the donut shop and caught a glimpse of Rochelle watching him. To Blake, he said, "If you find anything out keep me posted."

"Watch your ass, Marco. Don't be in the wrong place at the wrong time when those hitters show up at Genesis' door. It won't be long before they peck their way up to him."

"I can take care of myself." Marco hung up and headed inside the donut shop.

Rochelle saw him coming and held up a stiff hand. "You can't come in here unless you're wearing a mask."

Marco paused in the doorway. Two customers were inside. A mother and her daughter. They sat at a far table eating cupcakes and drinking coffee. Both looked up to see how he would respond. Marco reached in his pocket and pulled out his facemask. After putting it on, he walked to the counter to face Rochelle.

"Are you Marco or Mondo today?" she asked.

He smiled, then realized that she couldn't see it through his mask. "That depends."

"On what?"

"Are you Rochelle or Nina?"

Rochelle leaned over the counter a bit. "I'm whoever I want to be. When I want to be it."

Marco detected a hint of anger in her attitude. "Let me explain . . ."

Rochelle threw her hands up. "No need. We won't be seeing each other anymore. It doesn't matter who you are."

She backed away and walked to a cup dispenser. He watched her for a moment, then followed her. "What do you want with Genesis?"

She turned on him. "None of your goddamned business."

"You don't like him, Rochelle. I saw it in your eyes."

"You know me so well? After talking to me twice? After leaving me on a date?"

Just then, her co-worker Bobby came out of the back to find the source of the commotion, wearing the same tired and sweated-out facemask that he'd worn the other day.

Marco kept his voice low. "You didn't look at him the way you look at me."

Bobby stepped out and stood beside Rochelle behind the counter "Need me to take over for a few?" He glanced at Marco.

Rochelle told Marco, "Come on." Marco stepped behind the counter and followed her to the back. She entered a walk-in cooler. Marco hesitated outside. "Come on," she said. "No one will hear us in here." Marco stepped inside.

Once the door closed, Rochelle yelled, "You've got some fucking nerve trying to leave me in a restaurant by myself! Then you want to come in here and question me about what I want with another man. What kind of shit are you into?"

Marco didn't know what to say. If he told her the truth, it would blow his cover. If he lied, whatever he said would lead to another lie. That was no way to start a relationship. He had to be honest with himself. He did want a relationship with her . . . eventually.

"Rochelle, there's a lot that I can't tell you right now. I owe you an explanation, but . . . you don't know Genesis the way I do."

"He's a drug dealer? That what you want to tell me? You work for him, so he can't be that bad."

"Rochelle . . ." He wanted to explain, but an urge struck him that he couldn't ignore. He pulled down his mask and embraced her. He pulled down her mask when he was close and kissed her.

She resisted by trying to push him away with rigid palms against his chest, but he held on, and soon her protests turned to gentle caresses as her hands snaked around his neck and pulled him closer. They kissed like that for a long time, so long that the frigid cooler no longer felt cold.

When Marco pulled away, he said, "Rochelle, I'm sorry . . ."

She kissed him again. "Don't talk." Her lips pecked his neck. His chin. His ear. "Just fuck me."

Marco felt her hand rubbing the growing bulge in the front of his jeans. "Are you sure you want to do this?"

She pulled his jacket off his shoulders and let it fall to the floor. It had been so long since she'd been with a man. Her fingers trembled. Her knees felt like Jell-O, yet she needed to know if a man could make her feel the way Cotton did. "I'm sure."

He kissed her again. Her fingers dropped and opened her jeans. She pulled away and turned around. Marco watched with his mouth gaping open as she shimmied her pants down around her hips. His eyes graced the round humps of her fat ass and he hurried to get his own pants open. Soon after, his dick was long and hard in his hand.

"Rochelle, I don't have a condom."

"Fuck it," she said, backing up on him. "Just put that motherfucker in me. And you better not have the damn rona either." Rochelle reached back and gripped his dick. "It's so big." She jacked him in her hand for a moment before placing him at her opening. "Go slow at first, baby."

Marco couldn't believe what was happening. He'd driven to the donut shop anticipating an argument, not fucking in the cooler. He pushed into her gently and found her pussy murderously tight. He didn't think he'd ever been inside of a woman so tight. He gripped her hips and pushed harder, until he eased halfway in.

"Damn," she purred. "You feel so good. Put it all the way in."

Marco thrust his hips hard and forced his dick inside her. Rochelle let out a little yelp, then she calmed down as he moved back and forth, easing in and out of her. Her pussy was so hot, he buried himself deep inside of her with every movement, just to revel in her heat. He reached out and gripped her fat titties as they jiggled with their slapping bodies. Rochelle pulled up her shirt and yanked down the cups of her bra so that he could feel her hot skin. Her hands gripped his as he pinched her nipples. Not long after beginning, Rochelle's body got used to him, and she began to move with Marco, throwing it back, meeting him thrust for thrust. Marco hunched over and planted sweet kisses on her neck, her ear, and her cheek.

"My God, Marco. Fuck me good, baby. Just like that. Keep fucking me like that."

Marco lifted Rochelle's foot up on a short shelf to spread her open a bit more. He clenched her hips and started pounding into her roughly, fucking her so hard that it hurt him each time he hit her bottom, but he couldn't stop. The feel of her juicy ass slapping against his thighs drove him on.

"Marco! Marco! Marco! Don't stop!"

Rochelle reached between her legs and gripped his balls. The sensation made him fuck her faster. Rochelle cried out as she came and squeezed his balls tight. Marco kept fucking her, until she was out of breath and panting.

When she finished she stood up and turned around. She stepped close and grabbed his dick again, wedging him between her legs as they stood belly to belly. His hard dick slipped in easily. Marco grabbed her ass cheeks to hold her still as he pounded into her. Rochelle wrapped her arms around his neck and pulled him close for a kiss.

"I want to suck your dick," she whispered. "But not now. Next time, I'm going to suck you so good that you cum down my throat."

Hearing her talk nasty made the pressure build between his legs. He fucked her with long strokes that forced him to squeeze her ass tighter in his hands. She pressed against him so close that he could feel her nipples stabbing him in the chest.

"Ooo . . ." she squealed. "Keep fucking me like that and you're going to make me cum again."

The standing position was awkward, and Marco struggled to keep his balance. He held her tight as he fucked her, loving the feel of her hot pussy. Rochelle kissed him deeply again. He felt her hands slip down his back to grip his ass to force him to fuck her harder. Rochelle lost her breath again. She fucked him back, forcing his dick to slip deeper into her until her body went rigid and she came again. Marco held her close as his own orgasm threatened to send him over the edge. He kept his pleasure at bay until she was done.

Without a word, Rochelle dropped to her knees and took him in her mouth. She sucked him greedily, then swirled her tongue around his dick head when she pulled all the way back. Her fist jacked him furiously until he could take no more.

"Rochelle. Baby. Ease up." He panted.

"Shut up." She slurped him up again, sucking him in long and slow strokes that drove him wild.

Marco looked into her eyes as he came in her mouth. Rochelle buried him deep down her throat and massaged his balls as he came, swallowing every drop. Marco threw himself against a cooler shelf as he let go. When he was done, Rochelle sucked him a little more, letting him grow soft in her mouth as she looked up into his eyes. Then she pulled back and stood up.

They smiled at each other silently as they dressed, each remembering how the other felt.

When they were dressed, Rochelle held the cooler door open and they walked out. Before Marco stepped back out into the store, Rochelle told him, "Mind your business, leave mine alone, and we'll be just fine. But if you question me again . . . I'll kill you."

FIFTEEN

LACY WAS SEARCHING THE INTERNET for cheap apartments on her laptop when she heard Bunny slide her bedroom window up at half-past six p.m. Bunny climbed through, then pulled the window down to keep out the cold air. Bunny shivered, "It's cold as fuck outside!"

"Where have you been?" Lacy asked her. "I've been texting you all day."

Bunny peeled off her heavy coat and threw it on the floor before plopping down into the beanbag chair. A half-eaten box of pepperoni pizza rested on the nightstand. Bunny picked up the biggest slice and tore into it.

Lacy frowned and turned back to the apartment complex she'd found in College Park. Nine-hundred a month for a two bedroom. "That's pizza we ordered two days ago."

Bunny glanced at her food as she chewed. "You should have thrown it out yesterday." She took another bite. "But it tastes fine to me."

Lacy sucked her teeth. "Nasty ass white girls. You never answered my question. Where were you?"

"I met this guy."

Lacy looked over at Bunny and recognized the knowing expression on her face. She didn't have to ask what her and the guy had done. Maybe she met him while walking to the gas station. Bunny went back to his place. They smoked a blunt or drank a little liquor. Bunny didn't drink beer, so Lacy knew it had to be Gin, E & J, or Hennessey. He tried to talk to her. Bunny told him to shut up, and she let him fuck her from behind. Maybe they got high and she sucked his dick in the car. She sucked it real good so that he'd text begging for her to come over again that night.

"Where'd you meet him?" Lacy asked her.

"You remember my cousin, Stacy?"

"The fat little blonde? She's still in middle school, right?"

"She's a ginger like me. Sophomore at Redan High in Stone Mountain," Bunny reminded her.

Lacy did remember her. They took her to a party at Five Points once, in an apartment near Underground Atlanta. There were fifty guys there, and Stacy disappeared with four of them. She met up with Lacy and Bunny drunk, high, and walking funny. Ten minutes later, she left with four other guys. Bunny had to pull out her little rusty twenty-two just to get the guy out of her mouth and the other one out of her ass. Stacy still didn't want to leave. They had to drag her to the car.

Lacy looked back to her computer. "Yeah. I remember her. What about it?"

"Her mama went to jail for prostitution again."

Lacy smirked. "I'm glad you didn't bring her little fast ass over here."

"I wouldn't dare. She was at my house when I went in last night. I think she'll be there for a while. She was talking to this guy out in Adamsville. I talked to him for a minute. He turned me on to his homeboy who lives in Stone Mountain. He picked me up this morning. He wanted to take me out to breakfast. I told him to take me back to his place instead."

Lacy shut down her computer and turned to face Bunny. "He got some bread?"

Bunny nodded. "He was driving a Lexus when he came to get me. When we parked in the two-car garage, he pulled in next to a Mercedes 600E. Brand new. Still had thirty-day tags on it."

"Dope boy?"

"Gotta be."

"Cash?"

Bunny licked her lips. "He was into some weird shit. He kept asking me how old I was. I said I was nineteen, he kept saying he didn't believe me. He said I was lying. He made me tell him I was fifteen. Then he was talking about tying me up. We went up to his bedroom and he opened a drawer to show me all these ropes and handcuffs. Motherfucker had dildos and shit."

Lacy turned up her nose. "Tell me you didn't let him put one of those in you."

"Hell no. But when he opened that drawer—the one with all the sick shit in it—the one below it came open too. I don't know if he noticed, but I saw some money in there. A lot of money."

Lacy searched Bunny's eyes. Bunny wasn't interested in a boyfriend. She craved money and dick—in that order. Rarely did she sleep with a man for pleasure. Lacy knew that she'd been sexually abused so much that Bunny couldn't get pleasure from sex. Not anymore. Making money and extending her power over men got Bunny off. Allowing a man to fuck her gave her a level of control that she never had with the men who abused her as a child. It didn't matter if she got off or not. Fucking for her wasn't about getting off. If the guy had money they could steal—that was a bonus.

Lacy asked, "How much?"

Bunny smiled. "I don't know. Maybe fifty thousand or so."

"Fifty thousand?" Lacy thought about that. "How do you want to do it?"

Bunny's phone vibrated in her pocket. She pulled it out and looked at the number. "That's him. He's been texting me since he dropped me off thirty minutes ago."

Lacy laughed. "You must have some good pussy."

"I'd sell it if I could put it in bottles." They both laughed, then Bunny said, "I'll text him later and tell him that I'm coming to his crib. We'll go over there and take it."

"No mask?"

Bunny shook her head no. "Fuck it."

"You know what happens when he sees our faces. We can't let him talk to anybody."

Bunny shrugged. "Why stop now? We haven't been letting 'em live."

Lacy was silent for a long time. When they started robbing drug dealers a year ago, she never thought they would be forced to kill someone. It was something that was always in the back of her mind, but she never thought it would actually happen. She figured them seeing the gun was enough to make them give up the goods. She was wrong.

Bunny fired off a text. "I just told him that I'd come to his crib later tonight."

Lacy's heart quickened at the thought of getting paid. "Let's get that money."

"Who's money y'all getting?" Lacy and Bunny both looked to see Rochelle standing in the doorway with her hands on her hips. Lacy tried her best to turn away from her sister, but Rochelle saw her swollen eye anyway. Rochelle hurried into the room. "What happened to your eye?" She grabbed Lacy by the chin and forced her to look up. "I know you didn't let some nigga punch you in the face. Tell me you called the police."

Lacy shook free. "Ain't nobody punched me in the face. I slipped on some ice and hit my eye on the back of a car."

Rochelle pursed her lips. "Girl who the fuck you lying to?"

"Rochelle . . ."

Rochelle threw up her hands. "Whatever. If you don't want to tell me, that's your business. But don't come running to me when he stomps a hole in your ass because you're too hardheaded to listen to somebody."

"Nobody hit me, Rochelle. Damn."

Rochelle turned to Bunny. "And why are you in my house with no facemask on?"

Bunny shrugged. "I don't have anything. I don't go anywhere but here and home."

Rochelle shook her head. "Ain't no telling where your mama has been. I know that's your mother, but I've seen her wallowing in the gutter. I don't even want to talk about it. Shit, you might not need to go home."

Bunny's eyes lit up. "Can I live here?"

"You're already living here. You've got your clothes in Lacy's dresser. You eat all three meals out of my cupboard. You sleep and shower here. Damn, do you have another home?"

Bunny laughed. "I guess not."

Lacy looked to Rochelle. "You going to the club tonight?"

Rochelle spied her sly-eyed. "I might be. Why?"

"Can you ride with Cotton so me and Bunny can borrow your car?"

"Why ask now? You've been stealing it this whole time. Or did you think I didn't notice? I go to bed at two. Get up at six and half my gas tank is gone. A parked car doesn't burn gas, Lacy. Nor does it gain mileage."

Lacy's first instinct was to lie, but she knew that would only put her deeper in the dog house. If Rochelle had been logging her mileage, there was no way to lie out of it. She decided to try another deceptive tactic: the truth. "We have been taking your car. But we'll fill it up this time. I promise."

Bunny piped up. "Premium octane."

Rochelle shook her head. "I thought you were going to lie to me."

Lacy shrugged. "Why lie about it? I did it. You know about it. I didn't mean any harm."

Rochelle looked at her baby sister. "I'm glad you're finally growing up. But I wish you'd understand that I'm not out to hurt you, Lacy. I want to see you doing good. I don't mind you borrowing my car, but you have a habit of tearing shit up. If you can't treat my belongings with respect, you can't use them. Besides, if you would stay out of trouble, I'll give you the damn car. I've had my eye on a new car for a while now. When I get it, I'll use cash as a down payment and give you my old one."

Lacy raised her eyebrows. "Really?"

"Really. It's no different than what Mama did for me when I turned sixteen. She gave me a beat up Datsun hatchback. It didn't look worth a damn, but it got me where I needed to go."

Lacy tried to recall a memory of her mother, but the image escaped her. She had only been twelve when her mother died. It was a shame that she could barely remember her face, even from the few pictures they had of her in old photo albums that she hadn't seen in ages. Rochelle was the only mother she had ever known, so the sentimental story meant something to Rochelle, but nothing to Lacy.

Lacy said, "I guess we'll call a car to pick us up."

Rochelle huffed. "I'll ride with Cotton." She reached in her pocket and pulled out her car keys. "Are you going to see that boy that punched you in the face?"

"Nobody punched me, Rochelle."

Rochelle tossed her the keys. "You better be telling the truth. I don't want to have to kill me a motherfucker."

When she left, Bunny looked at her phone. "Shit. All that begging for nothing."

Lacy glanced to her. "What's wrong?"

"He just texted me. He said he'll be busy tonight. Maybe tomorrow."

"Fuck that," Lacy said. "We're going to get him tonight. It might be for the best that he thinks you aren't coming. This way, he won't know it's you, and we may not have to kill him."

SIXTEEN

MARCO SAT AT HIS COMPUTER replaying the video footage of the robbers leaving Devon Wright's house the night of his murder. He'd been over the footage a hundred times, and he didn't think he was any closer to figuring out who the robbers where than when he started.

The footage was so grainy that he couldn't make out the license plate of the burgundy car parked in front of Devon's neighbor's house. The masked figure ran into the frame and threw a small bag into the car before jumping into the driver's seat and pulling off. Seconds later, a white BMW sped by. Marco rewound the footage. Something struck him as odd about the way the robber moved, but he couldn't put his finger on it.

He paused the footage just as the white BMW sped by. In the right side mirror, he swore that he saw the fluff of a blonde afro, but he couldn't be sure. He rewound the footage all the way back to the beginning. He watched the robber run up to the car. He rewound it again. He watched that little section fifty times within two minutes.

His phone chimed. It was a text from Rochelle. *working tonite. can I c u in the a.m.? let u eat my donut this time?*

Marco laughed, thinking about their five minutes in the cooler. He replied, *didn't think i'd hear from u. miss u*

i'll text u when I get off. round three

ok

Marco put the phone down and had to focus to switch his train of thought back to his work. Each time he looked at the burgundy car, he thought of the burgundy car sitting outside of the donut shop where Rochelle worked. Hers was a Nissan Maxima. He looked closer at the car on the screen. The taillights resembled the taillights on the Maxima. He went to Google, pulled up a few images of various Nissan Maximas and thought he had a match with the 2012 model. He smiled to himself, happy that thoughts of Rochelle hadn't taken him so far from his work that he couldn't get anything done. She'd actually helped him out.

He kept watching footage of the robber getting into what he now knew was a Nissan Maxima. He watched it again and again, suddenly cognizant of the fact that had puzzled him before. He picked up the phone and called Detective Blake.

Blake answered on the fifth ring. "Yeah."

"It's Marco. Look, I was going over some of the surveillance footage you sent to my phone and I wanted to ask a question."

"What is it?"

Marco paused, not believing what he was about to ask. "What are the chances of the robbers being women?"

The phone was silent for a long time. Finally, Blake asked, "How did you come to that conclusion?"

"It makes sense. There was no sign of a break in at Wright's place. That means he let the robber in. He wouldn't let in a stranger. And let's look at the facts: He was found with his pants around his ankles, vaginal secretions on his penis."

"Maybe he was set up by a whore. I'll go for that, but it doesn't mean both of them were females. They could have used a woman to get in there."

"Or maybe they're both women."

Blake sighed through the phone. "If they were women, that means they're not likely connected to Genesis."

"So fucking what? It blows a hole in my investigation. That doesn't mean it's not true."

"Marco, the murders are connected to Genesis. Face it."

"Why do they have to be connected to Genesis? Because it plays into the narrative you want to give your bosses downtown? Got your eyes set on making lieutenant, huh? But at what cost? Ignoring the truth for something more sensational? What the fuck?"

"Calm down, Marco. We'll investigate it."

"No the fuck you won't. You want me to corroborate with your findings to lead you to a bigger bust. You're not satisfied with taking robbers and murderers off the street. You don't care about them. All you want is to reel in the big fish."

Blake laughed. "You think you know so much. All of them are the same. Robbers. Drug dealers. Murderers. Just more black asses filling up prison cells and cemeteries. You think I give a fuck? Yeah, I do want to make lieutenant. I want to run this city and run sorry ass niggers like Genesis out of it too. I wouldn't give a damn if the robbers were three-foot-tall midgets in tutus busting pop guns. They're killing the bad guys, and goddamn it, I'd pin a medal on their chests if I had the power. It isn't about them. It's about cleaning up this fucking dump and making it livable again. It's about getting the gangbangers off the streets. You monkeys are always hollering Black Lives Matter. Well guess what, pieces of shit like Genesis make a mockery of everything your people protest for. Go ahead. Turn on the news. Look at downtown. They're tearing it up. Why? Because niggers like Genesis give you all a bad name. Either you're going to help me, or you're not. But I'm going to clean up this city, even if I have to kill one dope dealer at a time. If the two scumbags that killed Devon Wright are going to help me by killing off pieces of shit, then so be it."

Marco grit his teeth. "You've got one more time to say the word nigger, monkey or anything close and degrading in my presence."

"It's just a fucking word, Marco."

"Yeah. A forty-five round is just another bullet. Until it punches through your goddamn face."

"Whatever," Blake commented. "Call me when you calm down."

"Calm down? Your views are totally racist. Have always been. They are based on racism, discrimination and stereotypes. White people break the law as well; people kill within their vicinity which means white people kill white people, Asians kill Asians, Arabs kill Arabs. . . You know what? Fuck you!"

Marco hung up and dropped his phone on the desk. He stared at the wall for a long time, hating Blake for what he said . . . and hating him for s showing his true self.

His phone rang again. He picked up without looking at the number. "Fuck you if you're calling to apologize."

"Apologize for what?"

He recognized the voice. But it wasn't Blake's. "Genesis? What's up?"

"It's two days 'til Christmas. I got you an early present."

Marco sat listening, hearing Blake's voice in his head echoing, *Niggers like Genesis give you all a bad name.*

"I'm into something right now. Maybe tomorrow."

Genesis laughed. "There is no tomorrow. There is only today. That's the mistake a lot of people make. They're always waiting on tomorrow. Get your ass over here." He hung up the phone.

Marco sat there, knowing that he'd been in the life way too long. He was tired of playing cops and robbers. He wanted to settle down with a woman like Rochelle. Somebody that made him feel good. Someone real. Someone he could come home to every night.

He picked up his pistol and stuffed it into the waistband of his jeans.

It was time to put an end to the bullshit.

SEVENTEEN

COTTON PULLED INTO THE TOWNHOUSE COMPLEX off Moreland Avenue in Five Points at a quarter to eleven. Rochelle sat in the passenger seat holding her pistol down low as she popped the clip to make sure it was loaded. Satisfied that she was ready to go, she slammed the clip home and stuffed the gun into her purse.

Cotton kept her eyes oscillating around the neighborhood, making sure no one saw what Rochelle was doing. "You straight?"

Rochelle nodded as she closed the top of the bag resting between her feet. "Always."

Cotton glanced at Rochelle. "Do you think he keeps money at his place?"

Rochelle shook her head. "Too smart for that. He just did a bid. He probably doesn't keep anything in the crib."

"This one is for free?"

"I told you to stay at home, Cotton. You chose to come out here. I told you what it was."

Cotton laid a hand on her thigh. "I wasn't complaining . . ."

"The fuck you weren't."

"Rochelle, what's wrong with you?"

Rochelle looked at her. "I need a change, Cotton. I'm tired of struggling. I'm tired of working two jobs that I hate. I'm tired of having a little sister who doesn't know how hard her life will be if she doesn't open her eyes and realize that the world doesn't owe anybody anything. I'm sick of this bullshit."

Cotton made a right down a short street ending in a cul-de-sac. A pink stucco townhouse sat at the crest of the circle with a Mercedes Benz G Wagon in the driveway. "We're here," Cotton told her.

Rochelle looked up at the townhouse and saw her mother's face looming above it. She never thought she would have the opportunity to avenge her mother's death. And now that the time was here, she was ready.

Cotton parked, and they got out. Cotton wore a tight black mini-skirt and a leather jacket. Rochelle wore black leggings, a long green sweater, and thigh-high leather boots. Both carried purses with pistols loaded to the max.

Before ringing the doorbell, Cotton looked to Rochelle and laid a soft hand on her shoulder. "Rochelle, I'll die for you. Don't question my loyalty or love for you. I know this isn't about the money. I don't care about money. I want you to put this nigga away so that you can bury your misery."

Rochelle didn't reply. She reached out and rang the doorbell.

Genesis opened the door wearing sweatpants, a T-shirt, and a smile. He looked the ladies up and down. "Goddamn, y'all look good. If I had known you were going to come dressed to impress, I would've cleaned up more." He stepped aside and let them in. Cotton walked past first. Genesis grabbed Rochelle by the arm when she tried to pass him. "Hey beautiful. Slow down. You're the one I wanted to see." He wrapped her up in a hug. When they pulled back, he lowered his lips to hers.

Rochelle allowed the kiss and desired to bite down on the tip of his tongue when he shoved it into her mouth. If she was thinking, she would have pulled out the pistol and did him right then, but she wasn't thinking.

The kiss ended. Genesis led them deep into his house. It wasn't extravagant by any means, but it was a decent place to live. They entered the living room. Genesis sat them down on one of two couches and asked, "Drink? Hungry?"

Rochelle shook her head.

Cotton said, "What kind of beer do you have?"

"Heineken."

She nodded. "Please."

Genesis walked off toward the kitchen.

As soon as he stepped out of earshot, Cotton turned on Rochelle, "Why didn't you do it at the door? The longer we stay here the more chances we have of somebody seeing my car . . . or seeing us.”

Rochelle stared ahead, her eyebrows clenched tight. “That would have been too easy. I want his ass to suffer.”

“Rochelle, you need to handle this shit and soon. When he comes back, clap his ass.”

As much as Rochelle wanted sadistic revenge, she knew that Cotton was right. It didn’t matter how Genesis died. Gunshot. Stabbing. Hanging. All that mattered was that he did die. She pulled her bag open and dipped her hand inside. There was already a bullet in the chamber. Rochelle flicked off the safety and waited for Genesis to return.

Rochelle formed a plan in her mind. She wouldn’t hit him as soon as he walked around the corner. She’d wait until he made it right in front of them. That way she was sure not to miss.

They heard the soles of his shoes clopping toward them before he rounded the corner. Rochelle’s finger tensed on the trigger. She had envisioned this moment many times, long before she thought that she would see Genesis again. She’d fantasized about it.

He kept his eyes on Cotton as he neared. “I kept it in the bottle because . . .”

The doorbell rang. Genesis paused ten feet away. Rochelle thought about popping him right then, but . . . who was at the door? It could have been a girl scout or a cop. Genesis kept toward them and gave Cotton her beer. Then he headed back to the front door.

Cotton and Rochelle exchanged glances. Neither had bargained on killing two people. Cotton stuffed her hand in her bag too. Rochelle knew Cotton had her finger on the trigger, ready to blast whoever came through the door with Genesis. All Rochelle had to do was set it off.

Then she saw Marco striding down the hall. Rochelle's heart stopped beating. Her hand slid out of the bag. She reached over and gripped Cotton's wrist. Cotton threw her a look, and Rochelle shook her head, no. Cotton eased up on her pistol.

Marco didn't smile as he entered. He sat on the other couch and kept his eyes forward. Rochelle tried not to look at him, but she couldn't help it. He glanced up just as she did. Their eyes locked for a brief moment, then they both looked away.

Genesis sat down beside Rochelle. "I'm sure you ladies remember, Mondo. He was at the club with me the other night."

Cotton licked her lips. "How could I forget?"

"Mondo, this is the surprise I was talking about. Nina and Cotton."

Marco sat back on the couch, keeping his eyes on Genesis. "How y'all doing?"

Rochelle leaned over to whisper in Genesis' ear. "I thought it was just going to be us three tonight?"

Genesis smiled and whispered back, "Mondo likes Cotton. Why not let them have a little fun?"

Rochelle looked over at Marco and thought about his lips on her neck as he fucked her from the back in the cooler at her job. She looked at Cotton and remembered how she pushed up on Rochelle in the bathroom, kissing her, fingering her, trying to get her to do unspeakable things that overstepped the boundaries of friendship. She couldn't understand the source of her jealousy. Was she upset because Marco was going to fuck Cotton, or because Cotton was going to fuck Marco?

In a way, it didn't matter. She only wanted to see Genesis dead, and it was evident that it wouldn't happen tonight. She didn't care who fucked who. When feelings were involved, everything turned out fucked up. The best thing she could do was push her feelings to the side and work her way back into Genesis' place for another night when she could kill him.

Genesis leaned over and whispered, "Look, I've got shit to do tonight. Why don't we go upstairs and . . . talk for a little while?"

Rochelle felt the heat from Marco's stare boring into her cheek. She fought the urge to look his way. "Okay."

She risked a glance at Marco as they stood up. He met her eyes, then looked away quickly. She knew he was upset, but she had no choice. If she killed Genesis tonight, she'd have to kill Marco too, and she couldn't bring herself to do that.

Genesis took her hand and led her up the stairs to his bedroom. Once inside, he closed the door and wrapped her up in a tight hug. He kissed her tenderly, as if they'd known each other for years instead of mere days. "Nina, you're something special. I've met a lot of women, but not one that makes me feel the way you do."

She pulled back a bit. "What way is that?"

"Like settling down."

"Are you serious?"

"I meet women all the time, but they want something from me. They think I have a little piece of change and they try to use me. You like me for who I am."

Rochelle raised an eyebrow. "I do?"

"You do." Genesis kissed her again. This time he slow walked to the bed as they embraced. He pulled the straps of her dress down over her shoulders. She wore no bra beneath. Genesis gasped at the sight of her naked chest. He bent down and sucked a nipple into his mouth. "Damn, you've got a pretty body."

Rochelle cradled the back of his head, wishing she could wrap her fingers around his throat and strangle the life out of him. Instead, she let the dress fall to the floor. Genesis pulled off his shirt, revealing a ripped body covered in black prison tattoos. TRUST NO ONE was scratched across his broad chest in cursive letters, framed by two pistols. Rochelle kissed his chest as he pushed down his sweat pants and stepped out of them. Rochelle tried to slip off her high heels, but Genesis whispered, "Leave them on."

As he lay her on the bed and climbed between her legs.

She felt his hand creep between her legs as he kissed her. She grit her teeth, hating that she was wet and ready to fuck. Her body had betrayed her. If anything she should have been a barren desert with him on top of her. Then she would feel the pain she'd felt all her life. From the loss of her mother. From the pain that he caused. Genesis pulled Rochelle's panties to the side and slipped his finger inside her.

Rochelle closed her eyes tight and was transplanted to the back of a courtroom where she sat alone. Genesis stood beside his lawyer, behind the defendant's desk, as a jury foreman stood and read the verdict. "We find the defendant, Genesis Hamlin, not guilty of second-degree murder." There had been an audible gasp from the audience. Perhaps the loudest from Rochelle herself.

She'd sat through the trial for two months. Had been forced to quit her job so that she could be there every day. She'd heard the evidence—what little there was—and prayed that they would convict him of killing her mother. But they hadn't. She didn't understand. Many people went to prison for crimes they didn't commit, but this man escaped prison for a murder he was so obviously guilty of. In the end, he was convicted of drug trafficking and sentenced to a decade behind bars.

Rochelle left the courtroom that day numb.

Almost as numb as she felt when Genesis pushed his fat dick inside of her. Her body responded to his touch. It became aroused. But she felt no pleasure. She kissed his neck. Kneaded his chest in her palms. She wrapped her legs around his midsection and held him deep inside of her, but she felt only hatred.

Instead of reveling in the passion of lovemaking, she could only think of the moment when she would kill him, and send him on his way for the transgression he had gotten away with. Thinking of revenge was the only way she could stomach letting him fuck her. The only way.

EIGHTEEN

THE HOUSE WAS A LITTLE ONE-STORY on Breeland drive in Five Points. Lacy drove past the place at half-past midnight. All of the lights were off. A blue Ford Expedition sat parked in the driveway. Lacy passed the house and parked up the street. Close, but far enough away that they could ditch the car and come back to get it in a few hours if they had to.

They got out with facemasks pulled taut over their faces, and their hair tucked. Bunny's wore her hair pulled back under a toboggan. Lacy pulled her Grinch hat down low over her ears to keep the chill from biting her flesh. She followed Bunny through the darkness to the back of the house. Bunny tried the back door handle. It opened on the first try. Earlier, Bunny told Lacy that she had left the door unlocked when she was in the guy's house. It was a good thing that he wasn't attentive enough to check it before going to bed.

The house wasn't as dark as it looked from the outside. There were lights on, most notably in the kitchen where they entered. Bunny tapped Lacy on the shoulder to let her know that she was turning it off. She flipped the switch, and Lacy followed her deeper into the house.

They walked up on a closed door down a long dark hallway. Bunny turned to Lacy with a rigid finger pressed to her lips. Lacy remained silent as they stood there listening to the faint sounds of music and moaning. Lacy swore that she heard R. Kelly's *12 Play* thumping from the room. She pressed her ear to the wall and listened closely. Somebody was in there fucking.

Bunny nodded to her. Lacy raised her nine-millimeter and nodded back. Bunny turned the knob on the door and pushed it open slowly. Sounds of slapping bodies echoed throughout the room. Lacy made out two figures fucking on the bed. The muscular body of a slim black man fucked a chubby white female from behind. The female didn't make moaning noises. It sounded like she was crying.

Bunny flipped the light switch. The guy rolled off the bed and reached for the drawer on his nightstand in one smooth motion. The white girl covered up with the blanket as her eyes struggled to adjust to the flood of bright light. Lacy hopped over a corner of the bed and stomped her foot on the drawer of the nightstand, trapping his wrist inside while training the gun between his eyes.

The man cried out in agony. "Okay! Okay! Let me go!"

Lacy kept her foot pressed hard on the drawer until Bunny moved behind him and pressed the barrel of her pistol to the back of his head.

"Slowly," Bunny whispered.

The guy peered up at them and pulled his empty hand out of the drawer.

Lacy kicked him in the face. He rolled onto his back, clutching his lips with one hand and his naked dick with the other. She opened the drawer and pulled out the chrome Desert Eagle inside. It felt like it weighed fifty pounds. She stuffed it into the waistband of her jeans. Lacy looked to the guy on the floor, then to Bunny. Bunny wasn't looking at him. Her green eyes were focused on the girl cowering on the bed. Lacy looked at the girl wrapped in the blanket.

The girl pulled the blanket tighter under their scrutiny. "Please don't hurt me."

Bunny walked close to the girl while Lacy kept the gun on the dealer. Bunny asked the girl, "How old are you?"

The child scrunched up her face. "You're a girl?"

Bunny didn't answer her question. "How old are you?"

The girl curled the blanket in the hollow beneath her chin. "Fourteen."

Bunny whipped her head around to the dealer, then back to the girl. "What's your name?"

"Bethany."

"Where do you live?"

"Across the street. I—I snuck out when Delbert called me."

"Delbert?" Lacy spat, jabbing the pistol in his face. "Your name is Delbert?"

Bunny asked, "How would your mama feel if she knew you were over here with Delbert tonight? If she knew what you were doing?"

"She would kill me. She wants to date Delbert too. Please don't tell her."

Bunny rubbed her eyes. "Can you keep a secret, Bethany?"

"I can if you will."

"Good. Don't tell anyone what you saw here, and I'll never tell your mother what I saw. Okay?" Bethany nodded. "Good. Now put your clothes on and go home."

Delbert looked up at Lacy. "Can I put some clothes on too?"

"Fuck you."

"I'm naked!"

Lacy kicked him in the face, making his nose explode.

Bethany hurried to dress in jeans and a sweat-shirt. She picked up her shoes and padded out of the room barefoot. Bunny stepped to the open bedroom door and listened. They all heard the front door creak open, then slam closed.

Lacy turned to Bunny. "That was stupid. You know the bitch is going to talk."

Bunny walked over to Lacy and Delbert. "She didn't see our faces."

"She heard too much."

Bunny shrugged. "Fuck it." She looked down to Delbert. "Where's the money?"

Delbert looked up. "Bunny? You shiesty bitch!"

She pointed the pistol at his face and said to Lacy, "Check the dresser drawer. Third one from the top on the left."

Lacy rushed to the dresser and opened up the drawer. She pushed aside an array of sex toys as she rifled through the drawer and came up empty-handed. She looked to Bunny who pointed her pistol at Delbert's face. "What the fuck? I thought you said he had money in here?"

"He did. I saw it. Check the other drawers. The one below the weird shit."

Lacy ripped out the drawer and spilled its contents onto the floor. Then she pulled out another, and another. She didn't find a dime.

Bunny cocked back and slapped Delbert hard across the jaw with the pistol. "Where's the goddamn money?"

"I don't have any money."

Bunny sneered, "You better find it quick, or your death will be long and painful. I don't mind leaving here with no money, but best believe that you won't leave here at all. You fucking child molester. I ought to kill you for that alone."

Lacy screamed, "FUCK!" Then she walked over to Delbert with her pistol locked on target with his face. "Where's the money?"

"I told you. I don't have any money."

Lacy looked to Bunny. "You got me out here for nothing."

"He had money! I swear!" She pistol-whipped Delbert across the face. He fell back. Bunny climbed over him and held him by the neck as she whacked him with the gun over and over again until blood stained the carpet beneath his head, and he begged her to stop. She squeezed his cheeks until his mouth opened, then she shoved the bloody barrel of her pistol inside.

With her free hand, Bunny yanked off her facemask. "Look in my eyes, motherfucker. Tell me I won't kill you. I hate you and men just like you. I don't give a fuck if you live or die. You do. When I pull back this gun, you better tell me something. I ain't playing with you."

Slowly, she eased the pistol out of his mouth.

Delbert's eyes bulged wide. "I sent my money out to re-up. Every penny. I swear."

Lacy sucked her teeth. "What kind of hustler gives his money up without getting product? That shit don't make sense."

Bunny feinted as if she was going to shoot him.

"Wait! I'm telling the truth. My man . . . Devon. That was my connect. Somebody killed him a few days ago. They sent some other dude to me. That's how he wants to do things. I give the money to somebody, then I get the product from somebody else the next day. What else am I supposed to do? I gotta eat. Niggas got their own ways of doing shit."

Bunny and Lacy exchanged a glance. Bunny looked back to Delbert. "Who's running shit?"

"I can't tell you all that. If they find out, they'll kill me, my mama, and whoever else I love."

Bunny pressed her pistol to the fleshy part of his face, right below his eye. "If you don't tell me, I'm going to kill you right now. Then you won't have to worry about any of it."

Delbert met Bunny's cold eyes. "His name is Genesis. I've only met him once. His cousin Jamal had a coming home party for him at his crib a few months ago. They say he's plugged in with some Mexicans. A cartel down in Juarez. I don't know. I went through Devon. Now that he's dead, some guy named Mondo called me. That's all I know."

Lacy turned the name over in her head. Genesis. "Where does Genesis live?"

"Not too far from here. Off Moreland Avenue. It's a pink stucco townhouse."

Bunny tapped the side of his head with her gun. "You better not be lying to me."

Delbert spied the gun from the corner of his eye. "I'm not. I swear. Just don't kill me."

Bunny looked to Lacy. Lacy shrugged at her, then she asked Delbert. "Are you sure you don't have any money in here?"

Delbert averted his eyes.

"We're leaving with a bag or a body. Your choice."

Delbert thought about that. "Under the bed. Nike shoe box."

Lacy ran over and found the box. Inside lay another pistol. A Lorcin three-eighty. The gun rested on top of a stack of bills. Lacy put the gun in her pocket and thumbed through the money. "How much is this?"

Delbert grit his teeth. "Fourteen thousand."

Lacy stuffed the money into her pocket and stood up. She looked to Bunny. "I'll be in the car."

Bunny nodded while keeping her pistol aimed at Delbert's face. Lacy walked out the door.

Delbert looked into Bunny's eyes. "I won't tell anybody that you were here. Just leave. I'll forget any of this ever happened."

Bunny stood up and shook her head. "You saw my face."

"Bunny, I was nice to you. I bought you something to eat."

"You raped that little girl." She twisted the pistol to the side.

Delbert threw up his hands to shield his face from the gun. "It wasn't rape. She . . ."

Bunny fired once. The bullet ripped through his forehead and punched a hole in the floor behind him as it exited. Bunny lowered the pistol to her side and watched his body go limp. She stood there for a moment, listening as his last breath escaped his body. She thought of how her stepfather, Patrick, used to creep into her room while her mother was off somewhere fucking some other guy. She felt Patrick on top of her. Slapping her. Telling her that she was a whore, just like her mother. Swearing no man would ever truly love her.

She thought of the men she had sex with willingly. Boys, adolescents, and strangers—some she could never remember their names, only shades of what they had once looked like when they fucked her young body mercilessly. She thought of the empty promises they made. Their smell. The hair on their chests. Their grimy fingernails digging into her flesh.

She raised the pistol once more. This time she emptied the clip into his face as she thought of all the men who had taken advantage of her and what she wished she could do to them.

Lacy had the car running when Bunny hurried out of the house and hopped in.

"I'm sorry about the money," she told Lacy.

"It's not your fault." Lacy pulled off quietly from the street and drove back toward the entrance of the neighborhood. "It was a good lick. Fourteen large is a lot of money. We good."

They pulled off their masks and rode in silence for the rest of the trip. A few minutes later, Lacy cut the lights and parked on the side of the road in a nice neighborhood filled with townhouses. The pink, stucco townhouse in front of them rested in the center of a large cul-de-sac. In the driveway sat a Mercedes Benz G Wagon. A Benz 600SL. And a little white BMW.

Bunny squinted at the BMW. "That looks like Cotton's car, doesn't it?"

Lacy shrugged. "You know how many white BMWs there are in Atlanta? Thousands. Ain't no way that's Cotton's car."

"Hmph. I guess you're right." Bunny stared at the house awhile longer. "You wanna go in there?"

Lacy shook her head. "Not tonight. We'll come back in a couple of days."

NINETEEN

MARCO WATCHED ROCHELLE FOLLOW GENESIS with his heart stilled in his chest. He couldn't believe it. They'd just had sex the morning before. Now she was going with Genesis. What was going on? They both had secrets. That was evident. She never told him why she wanted Genesis to think her name was Nina, and he never told her why Genesis called him Mondo, but he never thought she would sleep with him. The fact that she went upstairs with Genesis told Marco that Rochelle had a deeper secret, one he may never find out.

Cotton seemed as shocked as him. She sat silently as they went upstairs, watching with her mouth gaping open. And after they had been up there for a minute or two, she still sat silently on the other couch, staring at the stairwell, as if Rochelle would come bounding back down at any moment.

But Rochelle did not come back down. Ten minutes passed. Cotton yanked a scrunchy from her bag and pulled her afro into a tight ball at the back of her head. After that, she twisted her fingers in her lap, then looked to Marco. She stood up and walked to the couch where he sat.

"Is there another bedroom?" she asked Marco.

He nodded, but he didn't move to stand up.

"Do you want to . . ."

"Nah. I'm good." He wouldn't meet her eyes.

Cotton sat down next to him. "Look. They might be up there for a while. Maybe all night. Don't you want to have a little fun?" She crossed her legs and leaned his way so that her knee brushed his. "You're sexy as hell. You'll love rubbing on my ass and seeing what I can do with it."

Marco pulled back a bit. "Cotton, you're fine as hell. I don't know you, but I can tell you're smart. I just ain't feeling it right now."

She frowned. "Aren't you attracted to me?"

He watched as she jutted out her breasts for his pleasure. With her hair pulled back, he could really see how beautiful she was. "That's not it."

She leaned over, so close that her lips brushed his when she said, "Well what is it? I've got all this *good* pussy to give you, and you don't want it? I bet you've got a big dick." She thrust her hand between his legs and grabbed him there. "Ooo. It is big. Let me make it hard for you." She kissed him softly. Her lips were stained with a fresh smacking of lip gloss, sticky and sweet to the touch. Her hand rolled in circles around his crotch. "That's it. Let it get hard."

Marco leaned back into the couch. Cotton kept kissing him, harder this time. Her tongue stole inside his mouth and tasted of honey and fruit and everything sexual that made him want to feel how she felt inside.

"You've got my pussy so wet, Mondo." She took his hand and shoved it beneath her skirt. She wore no panties. Cotton guided Marco's fingers toward her wet slit and inside of her. "Goddamn it feels good to be touched like that," she whispered. "Rub it. Rub it good."

Her own hands fiddled with his fly until she had it open. She stuffed her hand inside and pulled his dick out. She started jacking him off right there on the couch.

"You've got a big ass dick," she said, her hips jerking off the couch each time his fingers touched her clit. "I want your dick in me. Hurry up."

"I don't know. I don't want to . . ."

Cotton kissed him again as she jacked him off. "I know you like Nina. I see the way you look at her."

"What?"

Cotton hiked up her skirt and threw a leg over his waist to straddle his lap. His hard dick protruded between their bellies. She shrugged her top down, exposing Double-D caramel breasts with butterscotch nipples. She watched Marco's lips tremble at the sight of her titties.

"I know you like her . . . rub my titties." Marco's hands cupped her breasts. "She likes you too." Cotton kissed him and grabbed his dick as she rose up on her knees. "She didn't have to tell me. I can see it."

"I like her, but . . ."

"It's okay," she said, rubbing his dick against her pussy. "Ooo shit. I like her too. But you've got to understand . . ." Cotton kissed him on the lips again. "She's upstairs fucking another man. So you might as well fuck the shit out of me." Cotton sat down on his dick and cried out as he shoved deep inside.

Marco wanted to push her off, but she felt so good that he couldn't stand to. Her arms snaked around his shoulders. She pulled him close as she rode him. His hands dropped to her ass cheeks and squeezed as she picked up pace. Soon, she was fucking him hard, slamming her pelvis into his. He felt her lips on his neck and all over his face. He tried to hold his pleasure, but he could not. He suckled her nipples as they came, each gripping the other tightly as the moment carried them away from demure thoughts of Rochelle . . . if only for the second that they felt pleasure.

Afterward, Cotton did not leave his lap. She sat there, stroking the back of his head, kissing him. She whispered, "Thank you." He was still hard inside of her, and she wanted only to catch her breath before riding him again.

That's when his phone chimed. "I need to get that," he told her.

Only then did she climb off. She lay back on the couch, watching him. The happiness of the moment seemed to fade away with their separation.

Marco fixed his pants and walked into the kitchen where he had a view of Cotton on the couch and the stairway where Genesis and Rochelle had ascended earlier. Hopefully he would see anyone nearing before they saw him. He called Blake.

As soon as Blake picked up, Marco whispered, "This shit better be good, after the way you were talking earlier, motherfucker."

"Calm down. I didn't mean anything by it."

Marco looked at Cotton on the couch. She was still lying there. Her legs were splayed open, and he saw that she was playing with herself.

"There was another killing," Blake said. "We know this guy was connected to Genesis."

"Who?"

"Delbert Ashland. A dealer out of Five Points."

"Goddamn. He was one of Devon's guys. I just sent somebody to see him this morning. Now he's on my team. What the fuck?"

"I told you, Marco. Somebody is picking off Genesis' guys one at a time. You need to watch your ass."

"When did this happen."

"An hour ago."

"An hour? That's not like our robbers. We usually don't find the body until the next day. They're getting sloppy."

"You're right," Blake admitted. "They left a witness this time. Seems Ashland was fucking an underage girl when the robbers burst in. They let her go. Her mama caught her sneaking in the house."

"Talk about a coincidence."

"Tell me about it. And get this. You were right. The robbers were female."

Marco's heart quickened. "How do you know that?"

"The girl spoke to them. Both were female. She was positive. And guess what else?"

"They rode off in a sleigh pulled by some reindeer?"

"No. The mother wrote down a partial of the license plate. She saw the car pulling off and chased after it. I've got a list of car owners to send to you . . . if you want it."

"Email it to me now."

"It's on the way. If you see something that jumps out at you, let me know. We need a break in this case. The sooner the better. And Marco . . ."

"What?"

"I'm really sorry about what I said earlier. I was out of line."

Marco thought about Blake disrespecting the Black Lives Matter movement. Marco was a Black cop, and he knew that the police brutality plaguing Black communities wasn't how things were supposed to be. "Fuck you." He hung up the phone.

A moment later, he got the email from Blake. His eyes scanned the list of possible owners of burgundy Nissan Maximas that matched the partial license plate number. It was a short list. Three. He zeroed in on just one. He stared at the name, thinking, *There's no way. Rochelle Jenkins?* He looked at the stairwell and thought about Rochelle getting her back blown out by Genesis. How could she be here, but her car be part of a robbery and murder? Her address was in Decatur, just off of Candler Road. He could make it there in a few minutes.

He looked out at Cotton on the couch. She was lying on her belly now, staring at him. Her fat, yellow ass poked up, beckoning him. He walked out into the living room regretting what he had to do, yet grateful that he couldn't continue what they'd started. They'd already gone too far.

"You have to leave, don't you?"

He nodded.

She stood up and walked to him. "I won't tell Nina about what we did."

"I'm not worried if you do."

Cotton reached up and wrapped her arms around his neck. "Yes you are. You want the same thing I want."

When she pulled back, he asked, "What's that?"

"You just want to be loved by someone."

He was cruising down Chandler Road ten minutes later when he spotted Rochelle's burgundy Maxima turn at a gas station. He slowed a bit, then followed. It was two thirty in the morning. Only a few cars occupied the roads. Whoever was driving would know they were being followed, so he followed at a careful distance.

The Maxima parked on a side street with the lights still on. The passenger-side door opened, and a short white girl hopped out. She walked to a rundown house with boarded up windows on the front façade. Marco wrote down the address as the Maxima pulled off. He didn't have to follow it far. The car turned down the next street and parked just two houses down from the intersection.

Marco cut his lights and slumped in his seat. The driver's side door opened and a young woman climbed out. She wore all black, except for a green Grinch hat. Marco thought about the hat. He'd seen Rochelle wearing one at the donut shop where she worked. He squinted into the night, thinking that the girl looked a little like Rochelle. She was much too old to be her daughter, but maybe she could be her sister.

The woman went into a one-level shotgun house and closed the door behind her. Marco waited a few minutes. He opened up his glovebox and found a little pill box with a GPS tracker inside. He'd planned to put it on Genesis' G Wagon, but he thought this would be a better use for it.

He got out and stole into the night. The car's hood was still warm when he laid his hand on it. He fished around under the tire well until he found a clean spot and taped the GPS tracker there. He hurried back to his car, hoping that the hunch he had about who was pulling the robbery-murders was wrong.

TWENTY

ROCHELLE'S RINGING PHONE WOKE HER at seven a.m. She answered. It was Bobby at the donut shop. "Look, my daughter tested positive for Covid. I can't make it to work—probably won't be in for a few weeks. I don't think I have it, but you can never be too sure. I'm going to self-quarantine."

Rochelle looked at the date on her phone. It was Christmas Eve. She was supposed to be off for the next three days. Her first stay-cation in months. She sat up and wiped sleep from her eyes. She and Cotton hadn't made it home from Genesis' house until four in the morning. The last thing she felt like doing was going to work. "You need me to go in for you?"

"Yeah. Cynthia will be there."

"She's a new hire. What is she going to do?"

Bobby sighed. "She's all I got. I think she can hold her own in the bakery. You just stay out front and handle the customers. You'll have a few bulk orders to fill, but other than that you'll be fine."

Rochelle muttered, "Oh-kay."

She stepped out of the shower five minutes later and realized that she was hungry. She threw a robe around her shoulders and headed to the kitchen to scramble a few eggs before dressing for work. Food might make her feel better.

Cotton was already in the kitchen when she entered, leaning against the stove chewing on a corner of a bagel. She wore a white terry-cloth robe this morning, tied tight around her middle. Her eyes rolled toward Rochelle and stayed there.

Rochelle opened the refrigerator and looked inside for the eggs, trying her best to ignore Cotton. They hadn't spoken on the ride home. Cotton had driven the streets of Atlanta with her eyes forward. Didn't say a word when they got in the house. Rochelle knew that she was upset, and she dreaded the moment when Cotton did say something. At the same time, she wanted to get it over with. She stood with the eggs and reached for a bowl from a cupboard. "Something wrong with your eyes, Cotton?"

Cotton smacked her lips.

Rochelle pulled out a fork from a drawer, then she began breaking eggs into the bowl. "You're not the type to hold your tongue."

Cotton threw her bagel in the trash and stalked over to Rochelle. "You're changing. Hiding shit from me. When did you start doing that?"

Rochelle beat the eggs with her fork and kept her eyes on the bowl. "What are you talking about?"

"That guy Mondo. You know him."

"You're crazy. I don't . . ."

Cotton dipped her head low to force Rochelle to look at her. "Don't fucking lie to me. I know you better than I know myself. I could hear your heart beating when he walked in the door. We could have killed both of those niggas last night, but you stopped it." She searched Rochelle's eyes. "Why?"

Rochelle put the fork down. "Because he didn't have anything to do with my mother's murder. Genesis did."

Cotton shook her head. "It's more than that. You know him. I can feel it. You like him, and he likes you too."

Rochelle wheeled around on her. "What business is it of yours? I'm not your girl. I am a grown-ass woman, and I can do whatever the fuck I want. You didn't have to come with me last night. I don't know why you wanted to go. It's not your place to kill Genesis."

Cotton stepped in front of Rochelle. "It is my business because I love you, Rochelle. I know you don't love me the same way. I don't care. But I'll do anything for you. Kill a nigga. Rob a nigga. I don't care. As long as it makes you happy." Cotton reached out and ran a finger down Rochelle's cheek. "Why don't you want me?"

Rochelle turned away from the tears pooling in Cotton's eyes. It's not that she didn't care. She cared too much. She realized that now. When she'd been lying in Genesis's bed, she felt none of the tenderness that she felt with Cotton. He was rough and manly. She found herself pretending that she was somewhere else. The fact that she was only doing it to get close enough to kill him didn't matter. Sex with most men was always unsatisfying. She often walked away feeling used, like some toy that had been discarded after a man played with it for a little while.

"Cotton . . ."

Cotton leaned in and kissed her. Cotton's breath tasted like candy canes and sugar. Rochelle resisted at first. Her hands rose to Cotton's cheeks to push her away, but Cotton held on. She wrapped her arms around Rochelle's waist and clutched her tightly—as if she would die if she let go.

Rochelle had never been kissed by a man so softly. Her resisting hands slid around Cotton's neck to complete the embrace. Cotton pressed closer, smashing her breasts against Rochelle's. They kissed like that for a long time as they gave into the moment.

Then Rochelle remembered something. "Where's Lacy?"

"She left earlier. I don't know where she went. But she's not here."

Rochelle felt her heart beating furiously—so hard that it might pound out of her chest—as she stared into Cotton's green eyes. Cotton reached down and opened her robe, revealing her plump caramel curves. She wore nothing beneath. Rochelle looked down at her body and couldn't stop her mouth from watering. She wasn't attracted to many women, but she was infatuated with Cotton's body.

Cotton reached out and untied the rope binding Rochelle's robe. When the rope slunk to her sides, Cotton slid her hands around Rochelle's back to squeeze her fat ass as she kissed her again. The kiss was deeper this time. Slow and passionate.

Cotton's lips kissed a trail down to Rochelle's breasts. She sucked a hard nipple into her mouth and slurped on it while kneading the other. Rochelle's gentle moaning coaxed Cotton to try her more. Soon after, Cotton's fingers dipped between Rochelle's legs and twisted her hot clitoris. Rochelle leaned against the countertop and thrust out her pelvis, her body begging Cotton to dig deeper.

Cotton responded by sinking to her knees before Rochelle. She kissed her thighs before nudging her nose against Rochelle's wet slit. Rochelle twisted her hand in Cotton's thick afro and pressed her pussy to her lips.

Cotton looked up at Rochelle as she stuck out her tongue and licked her just once. "I love you so much."

Rochelle looked down into Cotton's eyes. It wasn't fair the way she had treated her lately. She was not in love with Cotton, but they shared a bond that deserved more honesty. Rochelle didn't have to be in a relationship with Cotton to sleep with her. Yet she whispered, "I love you too."

Cotton's mouth made an O of surprise, then spread into a sly grin. Her greedy tongue began lapping at Rochelle's sopping wet pussy. She used two fingers to pull Rochelle apart so that she could pleasure her more.

Rochelle's body tensed at the sensation. "Suck my pussy. Suck it."

Cotton slurped Rochelle's little clitoris into her mouth until Rochelle purred in delight. Her hands climbed up Rochelle's body and squeezed her fat titties. She licked Rochelle's pussy in tight circles with her tongue, knowing just how to please her.

Rochelle threw her leg over Cotton's shoulder and was rewarded with a finger plunging in and out of her hot pussy as Cotton licked her. She closed her eyes tight, and all the frustration of forcing herself to fuck Genesis disappeared. The pain evaporated and was replaced with only pleasure.

She gripped the back of Cotton's head as the orgasm swept over her body. And although she knew it was Cotton between her legs, the face she imagined eating her out was Marco. Not Cotton.

Cotton stood up slowly. Rochelle kissed her deeply and spun them around so that Cotton's back was pressed against the counter. She kissed Cotton's neck, and down farther to her soft yellow breasts. Her nipples were light brown, like a caramel candy. When Rochelle sucked one into her mouth, Cotton pushed her back gently, "You don't have to do that."

"I do," Rochelle told her.

"No." Cotton shook her head and pulled her robe closed. "I don't want that from you."

Rochelle stared into her face. "What do you want from me?"

"I . . . I just want you to love me. Never leave me. Always be here when I need you." Tears fell slowly from her eyes. "I don't care who else you fuck. Just love me."

Rochelle peeled Cotton's hands from her robe and pulled it wide open. "I'm going to do that too." She knelt between Cotton's legs.

TWENTY ONE

ROCHELLE MADE IT TO WORK at eight a.m. Bobby had planned to open late on Christmas Eve. The Mexican girl, Cynthia, was waiting in her Subaru station wagon in the parking lot. She got out as Rochelle pulled up. They entered the store. Rochelle asked Cynthia if she knew how to prep the dough to begin making donuts, and Cynthia said that she was confident she could do it on her own. Rochelle told her to say something if she needed any help and left Cynthia to the baking. She had lots to do up front to get ready to open at ten.

Rochelle was dog-tired from her long night with Genesis, and longer morning with Cotton, but the routine work of filling cup dispensers, wiping down countertops, and setting up the cupcake displays kept her wide awake and busy. She had broken a little sweat by the time she finished her mundane tasks around nine o'clock. She was headed to the back to ask Cynthia if she needed help when she spotted Marco peering into the front door.

She walked over and unlocked it. "We don't open until ten," she told him. "Christmas Eve."

"I know," he said. "I'm not staying. I just—I just wanted to see you."

She stared into his eyes and regretted what she saw. "You're not mad about Genesis?"

He shook his head. "Not mad. Confused maybe. But we all have secrets."

The more that she looked at him the more that she thought he was lying. He was mad. Maybe not towards her.

She said, "Look it's nine . . ."

"I'll leave. I know you're busy."

"That's not what I was saying, Marco. I've got time." She looked behind her and heard pots and stainless steel dishes clanking in the bakery. "I don't want to talk here. Can we take a ride or something?"

Marco's eyes lit up. "Yeah. Sure. Anything you want."

"Stay right here."

Rochelle hurried into the back and shed her apron at the same time. Cynthia was pouring chocolate batter into cupcake pans. The bakery was spotless. She already had a load of cupcakes in the walk-in oven and several pans cooling in the corner. A big bowl of peppermint icing idled in the mixer. Rochelle was amazed that Cynthia had everything under control. She'd only been working in the shop for two weeks. She asked Cynthia, "You good?"

"Yeah, I'm good."

"Okay. I'm going to run out for a few minutes. Will you be okay?"

Cynthia nodded. "I should be."

MARCO WAS SITTING BEHIND THE WHEEL OF HIS BENZ when Rochelle stepped out into the freezing December morning. His car was already running, and the seats were warm when she slid in on the passenger's side. Al Green's "Simply Beautiful" played softly through the speakers.

He asked, "Where do you want to go?"

"Anywhere. Maybe you could park behind the strip mall."

Marco pulled out and drove around the back of the strip mall. Usually delivery trucks would be parked back there, but because of the holiday, his was the only vehicle driving through the narrow alleyway. He parked behind a dumpster so that he would see any vehicle pulling in before they saw him. He didn't think anything crazy would happen. It was just a force of habit. A cop habit.

Once parked, Marco turned to Rochelle. A million questions flooded his mind, but he didn't want to ask a single one. If she answered his questions, she'd expect him to answer hers. He wasn't prepared for that. Not now. Not when he didn't know what she wanted with Genesis.

He'd been up thinking all night long. He was positive that Cotton's BMW was the second car spotted at Devon Wright's house. He didn't think Rochelle's little sister was driving the Maxima that night. He couldn't prove it, but Rochelle was involved somehow. Maybe she set the licks up and her sister pulled the heists with the white girl. He wasn't sure, and he didn't think she would tell him if he asked, but he was positive Genesis was on her hit list. He hadn't told anyone . . . yet. He had no concrete evidence, and he didn't want a cop like Blake to fuck it up. For now, he kept what he suspected to himself.

"What do you want to talk about?" he asked Rochelle.

Instead of speaking, she leaned over the center console and kissed him. He sat stunned for a moment, allowing her to kiss him with his eyes wide open, but eventually he gave in. Not long after, her hands pulled open his leather bomber jacket and roamed over the contours of his broad chest.

He couldn't stop thinking about Rochelle and what she wanted from Genesis. It was obvious that she didn't like Genesis, but she'd climbed the stairs behind him. She'd slept with him. If it wasn't for pleasure, what was it for? It could only be to rob him. That fact bothered Marco, not because he didn't think it was possible, but because he couldn't see her robbing anyone. She was too sweet, too genuine, too beautiful.

Her hand slid down between his legs, and he stopped her from fondling his dick. "Wait a second. I thought you wanted to talk."

She kissed his lips again. "I did. Now I want to do something else." Her hand stole between his legs once more.

He gripped her wrist, but made no move to stop her from rubbing the growing bulge that she found. "It feels like you want to do something else too."

"Rochelle." She looked into his eyes. "Genesis, Rochelle."

She pulled back and stared ahead. "Why did you have to go and say that?" Rochelle jerked open the door. "I shouldn't have come out here with you."

Marco reached over her, snatched the handle and slammed the door closed. "Hold up."

"I don't want to talk about Genesis."

"Neither do I," he said, "but I don't know if I can do something with you without thinking about where you were last night."

She pursed her lips. "You don't think Cotton told me what you did with her?"

"It doesn't bother you?"

She leaned close to him again. So close that her breath beat against his cheek. "What do you think? We're all grown. We can do whatever we want. The key is knowing what you want. I want you. If you want me, I'm here. Take it. Don't think about what was, or what could have been. Accept what is and keep it moving." She kissed him again. This time deeper. Her palm cradled his cheek. She pulled back and looked into his eyes. "Keep kissing me like that, and you won't be able to tell me no."

An odd thought struck him as he stared into her eyes. He felt her passion, but also pain. Rochelle had been hurt in unimaginable ways. It showed in everything she did, every move she made. Someone had taken away something that she loved. They took it, and now she found it hard to love again. She gave herself to meaningless sexual trysts that did not involve love—as a protection—not for pleasure. He wondered what happened in her life to destroy her. But he didn't have to wonder who. It was evident to him now. Genesis.

He said, "My brother Chauncey was a hustler. He was older than me. My pops was a hustler too, but he died when I was young."

"He get killed?"

Marco shook his head. "Heart attack at forty-one. Ironic, huh? But once he was gone, Chauncey took it upon himself to provide for us. He was twenty-one. I was thirteen. He had cars and clothes. All the girls loved him. He bought me whatever I wanted. He'd come to mama's house in the morning with a pocket full of money. Some he'd give to mama. Some he gave me. Most of it he kept. I spent my childhood fantasizing that I was a hustler just like him. Then one morning he didn't come by mama's house. They found most of his body parts floating in a black garbage bag in the Chattahoochee river in Tennessee. The streets said that he owed somebody a lot of money and he didn't pay fast enough, and the two guys that he hired killed Chauncey."

Rochelle laid a hand on his thigh. "I'm sorry."

"That's the price of doing bad business."

"Did the men who did it go to jail?"

Marco shrugged. "Nah. Never got arrested. I grew up wanting to kill them. My every day was consumed with thoughts of killing them. But you know what? One of them was shot by the police during a botched robbery. And the other one was stabbed to death by his girlfriend after she found out he was cheating on her. I didn't get the satisfaction of killing them myself, but I slept better knowing they paid for what they did to Chauncey in some way. That's the thing about karma. It may not catch up to your enemies when you want it to, but it does catch up."

ROCHELLE LISTENED TO MARCO'S story with her heart beating wildly in her chest. She wondered how he knew what she was planning to do to Genesis. Hearing about the loss of his brother made her look at him in a new light. Here was a man that had been through the same thing she had. How did he cope? He was a hustler, but maybe living with the death of his brother made him a smarter hustler.

Regardless, Rochelle didn't think he knew that she wanted to kill Genesis, but he obviously felt something. She clutched his hand in hers. "I want to move away from here," she told him.

"Why?"

"There's nothing here for me anymore. I thought I would live in Atlanta all my life, but now, I never want to see this place again."

"When are you going to leave?"

"I don't know," she said. "My sister will be going off to college soon. She'll be on her own then, and I'll be free to go where I want. But I have to do something first."

Marco looked into her eyes. "I don't want to know what it is."

"I wouldn't tell you if you asked."

He kissed her lips. "Listen. I know we won't end up together. Our secrets won't let that happen. We'll only destroy each other in the end. Do you feel that?"

She nodded.

"Lie to me," he said. "I don't want to fall for you, because I know it can't work, but I already have. I just need you to lie to me."

"Lie to you about what?"

"Tell me that you're falling in love too so that I won't feel like I'm the only one. I know you don't care for me the way I care for you, but I'd like to hear it. Even if it isn't the truth."

Rochelle kissed him hard. Then she pulled back and looked into his eyes. "If I told you that, I wouldn't be lying."

TWENTY TWO

MARCO SAT BEHIND HIS LAPTOP with his mouth gaping open. He couldn't believe what he was seeing. He'd looked over Genesis' arrest record several times and never made the connection. How could he have been so stupid? Then again, he had no reason to suspect that Genesis' past could be connected to someone close to him.

First, he discovered the victim's name: Jackie Jenkins. She'd been a gas station attendant. On December 26, 2012, the Atlanta Chronicle reported that two unmasked men walked into a gas station and shot the owner, Michael Harris, at pointblank range in the face. Upon searching for the security equipment, one of the men found Jackie Jenkins cowering in a back storeroom. She had been shot dead with a single bullet in the heart. The killers never found the security equipment. The article reported that Jackie was survived by her two daughters: Rochelle and Lacy Jenkins.

Marco felt like a bloodhound on a flesh trail. He combed Google for other news and found footage of a series of interviews with Rochelle. The first was conducted shortly after her mother's murder. Rochelle stood on the porch of a rundown house in Decatur. She looked young yet aged from her recent turmoil. A little girl stood beside her with tears puddled in her eyes.

Rochelle's lips sneered like a lioness' before a fresh kill. "I will not allow these killers to get away with what they have done. They murdered an innocent woman. The police have their faces on surveillance footage and they deserve to die in prison. It's only a matter of time before they're caught, and maybe then me and my sister can see justice."

Another news story reported that Genesis had been arrested along with a second suspect named David McDougal. They were booked into the Cook County Jail on first-degree murder charges and both bonded out on five-hundred thousand dollars' bail shortly after. The irony of the arrest was that the DEA were forced to admit they had an open investigation into Genesis' drug dealing when he was arrested for the gas station murders. They didn't charge him with trafficking until months after he'd bonded out for the murder charge. By then, rumors circulated that David McDougal was the shooter acting on Genesis' order.

The only person who could prove that was David McDougal.

Police found McDougal strangled to death outside the Coca-Cola museum days before trial.

During Genesis' trial, the State showed the gas station's security footage. It was disappointing at best. It showed Genesis and McDougal entering the gas station, but the angles were off. No actual murder was captured on tape. The cameras had only caught McDougal with a gun and Genesis talking to someone off screen. Jackie Jenkins was killed in a storeroom without witnesses. With McDougal dead, the State of Georgia had no real case against Genesis. The jury was forced to find him not guilty. A week later, Genesis was convicted in a federal court of drug trafficking and sentenced to ten years in prison. Genesis left the courtroom with a smile.

Rochelle's last interview depicted a heartbroken woman with no one to turn to. She sat on the same porch with the same little girl behind her. With tears in her eyes, she told the camera, "Now what am I supposed to do? I'm not even legal yet. I have to raise my sister and make sure she has a place to rest her head and food in her belly. I have to be the responsible adult, but the man who killed my mother doesn't have to live with what he did, because the State is too incompetent to convict him."

Marco thought about the conversation he had with Rochelle in his car that morning. She said that she wanted to leave town, but she had to do something first.

He thought about the drug dealers' murders. There was no way that Rochelle had committed the last one. He was with her at Genesis'. But was she responsible for the other killings? It made sense. A scorned daughter killing drug dealers to avenge her mother's murder wasn't a far-fetched motive. But if she had him as an alibi for one, did she commit the others?

Thinking in circles gave him a headache.

His phone rang. It was a FaceTime from Blake. "Marco. Find anything on your theory about the robbers being women?"

Marco shook his head. "I'm at a dead end."

"You had it all figured out a day ago. What changed?"

"Everything. Look, I've got something to do. I'll hit you up if I find anything."

He threw the phone on his desk after hanging up. He couldn't tell Blake about Rochelle. Not yet. He didn't have enough evidence, and he didn't want to jump the gun. What if she had nothing to do with the murders. If she planned on killing Genesis, he would know.

He called Rochelle. "How are you?" he asked.

"Better."

"Can I see you?" he asked.

"Not tonight," she said. "What are you doing, anyway?"

Marco rubbed his eyes. "Nothing. Holed up at home tonight. Don't feel like wearing a facemask or spending money. I'm chilling at the crib."

"Will you dream about me when you sleep?"

Marco smiled. "I'll try." He paused. "Hey look. Remember that thing you said you had to do before you leave town?"

"Where are you going with this?"

He hesitated. "You don't have to do it. You can just pack up and leave all of this behind you. It's not as important as you think."

It took her a long time to answer. "Yes, it is." She hung up.

Marco stared at his phone for a long time after, resisting the urge to call her back. The last thing he wanted to do was stay at home. He wanted to be curled up in her arms . . . perhaps the arms of a killer.

He clicked on to the app that monitored the tracker on Rochelle's car. It had moved from her house and was headed toward Moreland Avenue in Five Points. Genesis' house.

Marco hopped up and stuffed his pistol into his waistband. He slung his jacket on as he headed to the front door, then he dialed her number as he was striding to his car.

The phone rang and rang, but Rochelle didn't pick up.

TWENTY THREE

COTTON PULLED HER BMW INTO GENESIS' DRIVEWAY and parked behind his G Wagon. It was eleven thirty at night. She looked over at Rochelle who was checking her nine-millimeter. Once Rochelle was sure that her pistol was loaded, she slammed the clip in and racked the slide to chamber a round.

Cotton looked up at the house. "You sure you're ready this time?"

She met Cotton's eyes after stuffing her pistol into her purse. "I'm sure."

"What if your boy Mondo shows up?"

"He won't."

Cotton blinked at her. "What if he does?"

Rochelle grit her teeth. "Jehovah couldn't save this nigga tonight. If Mondo tries to stop me, then Mondo has to go too."

Cotton nodded and plucked her purse from the backseat. She had checked her gun before they left the house. She looked over to Rochelle before climbing out of the car. "When this is over, where are we going?"

Rochelle leaned over and kissed Cotton on the lips. "We can go wherever you want to."

They got out and walked to Genesis' front door. Across the street an older white woman unloaded bags of groceries from her trunk. She looked over at Rochelle and Cotton as they stood illuminated beneath Genesis' porch light. The girls did their best to shield their faces. An innocent bystander could turn into a potential witness.

Genesis answered after they rang the bell. He smiled at Rochelle as soon as his eyes landed on her. He swept her up in his arms and kissed her. Rochelle squealed in mock delight. They all went inside when he put her down.

Genesis led them to the living room saying, "I was cooking dinner when you called. Are you hungry?"

Rochelle stuffed her hand into her purse. Genesis walked a pace in front of her. She wanted to pull out and pop him in the back of the head, but she wasn't sure if the woman across the street would hear the shot. If she waited a few more moments, she could kill him and leave without arousing suspicion. The woman would probably be safely in her home by then. She told Genesis, "I'm starving. What are you cooking?"

"Chicken parmesan. I learned how to make it in prison."

"Prison? How'd you learn how to . . ."

Marco was sitting on the couch when they entered the living room. He stared up at Rochelle as soon as she came into view. His eyes were hard on her, like he knew what she was planning. She removed her hand from her purse.

She sat on the couch adjacent to the one he sat on. "Thought you were staying in tonight." Cotton sat beside her.

Marco still wore his jacket. "Changed my mind."

Cotton leaned in close to Rochelle's ear and whispered, "Remember what you said. Not even Jehovah . . ." Rochelle nodded along, but looking at Marco made her realize that she couldn't kill him. No way.

MARCO KEPT HIS EYES ON ROCHELLE. He noticed how she clutched her bag close to her chest and knew that she held a gun in there. She had come to kill Genesis. He was sure of it. A part of him wished he had stayed at home and let it happen. He didn't give a fuck about Genesis. He cared about what happened to Rochelle. If someone was going to kill Genesis, it wouldn't be her. Not as long as he had breath in his body.

He noticed the front door open as he watched her. It opened slowly, as if it had not been closed and the pressure of the wind pushed it ajar. He glanced at Rochelle. She had her hand in the bag now. Cotton stuffed a hand in her bag too. Genesis went on about how he had taken a culinary arts class in prison and learned to cook all kinds of food.

Marco looked back to the front door. Two slim figures dressed in all black silently slipped into the house and pressed the door closed behind them. Marco whipped out his pistol and hopped to his feet. Rochelle and Cotton followed suit just as Marco pointed down the hall toward the front of the house. "Robbers."

Genesis jolted to his feet, oblivious of the fact that both Cotton and Rochelle held pistols. "What?"

Marco looked at Rochelle and Cotton standing with the pistols down at their sides. His declaration of robbers had saved his life. Rochelle looked upon him with regret, as though the first bullet would have been on a course for his face if he had not sounded the alarm. He kept his voice low. "Two robbers just came inside. They went upstairs."

Genesis glanced at Rochelle and Cotton. He pulled up a couch cushion and wrapped his hand around the butt of a chrome forty-five. He racked the slide. "They're about to die." He started toward the hallway leading to the front of his house.

Marco followed at a distance, looking beyond Genesis, who walked forward as if he did not fear death. He glanced behind him. Cotton and Rochelle seemed to argue silently, gesturing with their eyes in abandonment of whatever plan they had previously concocted.

Genesis paused at the threshold of the hallway. "We know you're in here. You've got two seconds to get the fuck out of my house. One . . . Two . . ."

One of the masked figures hopped down from the stairs and fired down the hall into the living room as they bolted to the other side of the hallway. Genesis dove behind the wall.

Cotton squeezed in behind Genesis. Marco crouched on the other side of the opening with Rochelle huddled at his back.

Rochelle whispered, "What the fuck is happening?"

"Somebody's trying to rob Genesis."

She didn't say anything else. Marco risked a peek down the hallway and spotted one of the robbers reaching for the door handle. He figured out the plan in a second. They'd snuck in expecting easy pickings. Now that they were caught, they were looking for a way out. The second robber hopped down the stairs and shot to make them all hide so they could open the door and escape.

Genesis picked up on the robbers' escape plans too. He peeked out and saw the same thing. Instead of allowing them to leave, Genesis raised his pistol and fired down the hall, punching a fat hole in the center of his front door. The robber yelped and rolled out of sight. The other one popped out from the stairwell aiming a pistol and licked off three quick shots in retaliation.

Before Marco retreated, he caught a glimpse of the green Grinch hat that one of the robbers wore. He glanced at Rochelle unconsciously, then he looked back and asked Genesis, "What the fuck are you doing?"

Genesis clutched his forty-five tight in his right hand as he hugged the wall. "They tried to rob me."

"They're trying to leave now. Let them go."

Genesis shook his head. "Fuck that. Don't nobody rob me. They been killing my niggas and shit. Ain't no way I'm letting them live tonight."

"Genesis," Marco tried again. "Let them go."

He shook his head again. "I ain't letting nothing go!" He peeked around the corner and fired off a round.

The robbers returned fire with a volley of their own.

Genesis pressed into the wall with a slight grin on his face.

Marco looked toward the back of the living room. He spotted a sliding glass door leading to the backyard. "Rochelle," he whispered. "Go out the back door."

"Why? Who are those people?" she asked.

Marco looked her in the eye. "It's your sister."

"Lacy? What are you talking about? Why would she be here?"

"The robbers are your sister and her friend. They've been pulling licks while driving your car."

Rochelle gripped her pistol tighter. "How could you know that?"

He regretted the words before they came out of his mouth, but he owed her the truth. "I'm a cop, Rochelle."

Her mouth dropped wide open. "A cop?" She glanced over at Cotton who watched her with curious eyes.

Marco said, "I'm sure it's your sister. The best thing you can do is go out the back door, circle around the front, and open that door so your sister can get the fuck out of here." Her eyes locked on Genesis. "Rochelle. What's more important to you? Killing him or making sure your sister is safe?" She met his eyes again. "If you don't go out that door and help her, she's going to die. Your revenge won't matter then. He will have taken two people you loved. Go."

Rochelle didn't need to be told again. She got up and hurried to the sliding glass door at the back of the house.

Genesis watched her and asked Marco, "Where the fuck is she going?"

"She's scared."

Cotton watched her too, but she didn't say anything. The murderous look in her eye said it all. She looked like a woman who felt that she'd been betrayed in some way.

Rochelle got the sliding door open and disappeared into the darkness outside.

Genesis looked down the hall, leading with his pistol. "I'm tired of this shit." He yelled out, "I don't know who you motherfuckers are, but you're gonna die today!"

Marco stared at Cotton. She raised her pistol and aimed it right at the back of Genesis' head. Marco leveled his gun at her face. "Cotton, no!"

She hesitated long enough for Genesis to look back and see her intentions. Genesis knocked the gun from Cotton's hand with an arching elbow, then he punched her in the face. When she fell back, Genesis climbed on top of her and pressed his gun to her temple. "The fuck you doing, bitch? Trying to kill me?" He gestured down the hall. "You with them niggas?"

Marco hopped up and ran behind Genesis. He aimed his pistol down at Genesis' back. "Let her go, Genesis."

Genesis peered up behind him. "Mondo? This bitch tried to do me."

"Let her go!" Marco jabbed the pistol hard into the back of Genesis' head.

Genesis laughed. "Fuck that. You ain't gonna kill me." He turned back to Cotton.

Marco pulled the trigger, catching Genesis at the base of the neck. Genesis cried out as his muscles tensed. His shock from being shot forced him to squeeze his own trigger, scattering Cotton's brains all over the floor with a single shot to her forehead. Genesis' body slumped on top of Cotton's.

Marco knelt down wand reached for his cell phone. He dialed 911. "This is Detective Marco Rawlings. I need an ambulance ASAP at 227 Mal à Suerte Lane . . ." He looked up and saw Rochelle standing in the front doorway. The two figures dressed in all black stood there too, staring down the hall at him. All of their eyes were locked on Cotton's motionless body.

Marco hung up the phone and yelled, "Get out of here! Go! Ain't nothing you can do for her now! Go!"

All three ran out the front door and into the night.

TWENTY FOUR

THE INTERROGATION ROOM WAS FREEZING COLD. Marco sat in a business suit with his badge pinned to the outside of his breast pocket. Two Internal Affairs officers sat across from him. One, Johnson, was a middle-aged black man. The other, Beaufort, was a slim white guy with a balding head and a bad acne problem. Johnson thumbed through a fifty-page sworn statement written by Marco. Beaufort stared at him while chewing a piece of gum that had to have gone stale fifteen minutes after they entered the room two hours prior.

Marco said nothing. His suit itched beyond belief, but he made no move to scratch. To show his discomfort would mean admitting weakness. He needed to project strength in this moment of turmoil.

Johnson closed the brief and sat back with his eyes scrutinizing Marco. "A harrowing tale. Too bad it's a bold-faced lie."

Marco said nothing. He gave nothing. He knew his statement had holes, but it was coherent and it would hold up in any court of law. He knew because he'd testified in over two hundred trials. He was a good cop. There wasn't a court this side of the globe that would doubt his word.

Johnson interlaced his fingers and rested his hands on the table separating them. "I didn't come all the way down here on Christmas fucking day to hear this bullshit, when I could have been at home hearing my kids' bullshit while they opened the too-expensive gifts I bought them. Tell us the truth. What happened to the money?"

"What money?"

"By the account of your own sworn statement, you were undercover for over two years. Yet you only turned in twenty-thousand dollars as evidence. What happened to the rest of the money?"

Marco tensed. "I was given instructions by my superiors to live as the dealers lived. That meant using drug money to support myself. I bought a Mercedes. Rented a spacious house. I bought expensive clothes. I did all of the things the dealers that I was investigating expected me to do."

Beaufort pinched his nose. "Wasn't your salary enough? Or why didn't you request funding from the department?"

"I could barely pay my bills with a detective's salary, much less live like a semi-rich drug dealer. And have you ever requested money from a state agency? It would take two months to survive a requisition for a pair of shoelaces. Be for real."

Johnson sat back. "What about this woman?" He opened the file. "Meghan Moore. Did you engage in a sexual relationship with her?"

Meghan Moore. Cotton.

Marco recalled an image of Cotton as she rode him on Genesis' couch. "That's irrelevant."

"You slept with her." Beaufort said. "It's a small detail. Admit it. We can't hold it against you."

Beaufort was lying. If he admitted to having a sexual relationship with Cotton, it would establish a motive for him shooting Genesis. Perhaps it would present a love triangle that would remove Marco from his neutral role as a law enforcement officer. The last thing he needed was a personal reason for physically harming Genesis.

"I never had sex with her. As far as I know, she had a sexual relationship with Genesis. I can't tell you anything else."

Johnson nodded along. "Who else was in that house? Forensics found bullets from two other guns shooting from the front door."

"It's like I wrote in my report. Me, Genesis, and Meghan Moore were in the living room about to eat dinner when two masked men entered the home. I spotted them, drew my weapon and fired at them. They returned fire. Genesis returned fire while accusing Moore of setting him up. I turned my weapon on Genesis and tried to arrest him. He shot Moore. I shot him. That's what happened. The robbers saw their chance and escaped. I never saw their faces."

Beaufort chuckled. "What about the neighbor? Betty Mandrake? She wrote an affidavit stating that she saw two women exit Moore's BMW and walk into the house. When questioned further, she was adamant that she saw two women. Not one."

Marco shrugged. "I can't control what witnesses see. They are not trained law enforcement officers. My statement says that Moore was the only woman in the house. I won't change it. That's the truth."

Beaufort leaned over the desk. "You're hiding a lot of shit. You may think you're smarter than us, but we'll catch you. The one thing I hate most is a dirty cop. You've fraternized with drug dealers for way too long. You took their money. You lived their lifestyle. You even smell like them. You've probably got dope stashed away somewhere. Money too."

Marco sat back in his seat. "What are you accusing me of? Being the stereotypical black male that you want me to be? Fuck you. I've been a law enforcement officer for eleven years. Eleven. Fuck yourself if you don't like it."

The door swung open. Blake walked in and surveyed the room. He laid his hands on Marco's shoulders and asked Beaufort and Johnson, "Is everything squared away?"

Beaufort stared hard into Marco's eyes. Then he nodded.

Johnson sucked his teeth. "Your boy is clean. Congratulations."

Marco stood up. The inquisitors stood too. Beaufort held out his hand for a shake. Marco looked at the hand as if he'd rather spit on it. He told Beaufort," Kiss my black ass."

Blake led Marco out into the hallway. Beaufort and Johnson remained in the interrogation room. Once they were down the hallway, Blake grabbed Marco by the elbow and stopped him. "You blew my promotion."

"What are you talking about, Blake?"

Blake pointed in his face. "You know what I'm talking about. Genesis had his house wired to the teeth with security cameras, and guess what? His hard drive was wiped clean by the time we got there. Not a single second of your shootout was recorded. All of the footage from neighbors' security cameras came up missing too."

Marco shrugged. "Are you implying that I dumped Genesis' hard drives? That's tampering with evidence—a punishable offense. I could go to jail for that. To make that kind of accusation, you'd better be able to prove it."

Blake laughed sarcastically. "I don't know who you're protecting, Marco, but I hope they're worth it. Because if I find out that your version of events doesn't wash out, you're going to be in a cell next to Genesis."

Marco started down the hall alone. He stopped dead in his tracks. "A cell next to Genesis?" He asked incredulously.

"Yeah, the fucker is in the hospital. He survived. For now anyway."

"You don't have to worry about me anymore." He took off his badge and slung it at Blake. "I quit."

Blake called out, "Merry fucking Christmas to you too!"

TWENTY FIVE

ROCHELLE AWOKE IN COTTON'S BED. The warm sun streamed in through the window, bathing her in a luminescent checker of light. She turned onto her back and stared up at the mirror on Cotton's ceiling. Whenever she laid down in Cotton's room staring back at herself while laying down had always made her smile. Not now.

After a while, an image of Cotton materialized in the reflection. She looked like a white chocolate candy on top of her black silk sheets. Rochelle saw Cotton's broad afro spread out like a cloud on the pillow beside her. Cotton smiled as she traced circles over Rochelle's brown skin. Rochelle stared up at the mirror, trying her best to keep the picture foremost in her mind, but it faded away, just like life from the body of her friend.

Rochelle rolled over so that she wouldn't see her own tears falling from her eyes. The silk pillow case was soft against her cheek, as soft as Cotton's lips had been. Each time she closed her eyes, she remembered how tenderly Cotton had kissed her. How she loved her. The tears came harder when Rochelle realized that she had not treated Cotton nearly as well as Cotton treated her. She'd been mean and spiteful. She'd taken advantage of Cotton's love—had taken it for granted.

Now her love was gone.

Rochelle was left with a hollow hole in her heart that could never be filled by another.

She felt a foreign weight on the other side of the bed. She rolled over and spotted Lacy sitting there with her head buried in her hands. Gentle sobs seeped from her. Rochelle felt the urge to reach out and hold her, but she didn't. She merely turned her back and stared at the wall.

"I'm sorry," Lacy sobbed.

Tears dripped from Rochelle's eyes harder, drenching the pillow. She said nothing.

"I know we haven't talked about it, but I am. Nothing I can do will ever bring Cotton back. Nothing. I—I just can't believe it. If I had never tried to rob that guy, she would still be alive."

Rochelle tried to erase the shootout at Genesis' house from her mind, but she couldn't. First, she still couldn't believe Marco was a cop. He talked like a hustler. Was as smooth as a hustler. He even smelled like a hustler. How could he have fooled her? Then again, he had no idea that she was a crook, so deception proved to be something they had in common. Yet, he was unforgettable. She would meet a thousand men and never meet one that made her feel like Marco did.

"Rochelle?" Lacy asked. "Why do you have your bedroom all packed up? Are we moving?"

She closed her eyes and saw Cotton squatting beside Genesis with a gun in her hand. Cotton had been sending silent signals, asking Rochelle if she should go ahead and shoot him while she had the chance. Rochelle shook her head because if Cotton shot and killed Genesis, she would have to shoot Marco, and that was something she knew she couldn't do, even though she had earlier promised that she would.

After Marco told her that Lacy was one of the robbers and she had fled through the back door, she circled around to the front of the house. No neighbors were outside, but she spotted a few looking out their windows, no doubt alarmed by the thunderous clap of gunfire erupting in the night. She'd crept along the front of the house and noticed a fist-sized hole punched through the front door. She'd eased along the side of the door and twisted the knob, pushing it open.

"Lacy," she'd hissed. "Get your ass out here!"

Lacy stumbled through the door with a pistol in her hand. Rochelle didn't need to see her face to know how her sister moved. Lacy looked to Rochelle and asked, "What are you doing here?"

"Saving your motherfucking ass! Now get over here!"

Bunny followed, but instead of running off into the night, Bunny paused on the sidewalk, peering back through the open doorway. She seemed not to fear any potential gunfire.

Rochelle said, "Bunny! What are you doing?"

Bunny kept staring. "They're fighting in there. I think—I think I heard Cotton scream. That was Cotton I saw, right?"

Rochelle hurried beside Bunny. The girl was right. She saw Cotton sprawled out on her back with Genesis straddling her. He had had a pistol pointed at her head. Marco stood poised above him, yelling, "Let her go!" Her heart told her to run inside, but her feet made her move in slow motion, creeping into the foyer as Marco and Genesis argued.

The gunshots made her stop. The first gunshot tore into Genesis' neck. His muscles flexed like he had been lifting weights. Then his gun went off, forcing Cotton's head to bounce off the floor. Rochelle's knees gave out. Lacy held her up and yelled, "Come on, Rochelle! The police are coming!" She faintly heard sirens echoing in the distance. Whether they were growing closer, she couldn't tell. All she could think about was Cotton and her dead body bleeding on the floor.

Her last thought before Lacy and Bunny shoved her into the passenger side of her own Nissan Maxima was: *She died trying to help me.*

Behind her on the bed, Lacy asked, "Rochelle? Are we moving?"

Rochelle rolled to a sitting position but still didn't face her sister. She hunched over her knees feeling tired. She'd slept a little, surprisingly, yet she felt exhausted. Her eyes hurt. Her body hurt. But nothing hurt more than her heart. "Lacy, I've done everything I could to raise you the right way. I didn't always do things right. I broke the law. But I didn't do it because I wanted to. I did it to make sure you had a roof over your head. Food to eat. Clothes on your back. All I asked was that you did well in school and went to college to make it easier on yourself. Not me. *You.* I can't help you if you don't even care about helping yourself."

Lacy was quiet for a moment. Finally, she asked, "What does this have to do with your stuff being packed?"

A fresh volley of tears streamed down her face. "You have to find your own way now. I can't take care of you anymore. I've done all I can do."

Lacy hurried to Rochelle's side of the bed. She sat down beside her. "I didn't mean for Cotton to get killed! I didn't know you two were even in the house."

"This is not about Cotton! It's about you needing to grow up!"

"I'm going to go to school, Rochelle."

Rochelle shook her head. "It's too late for that now."

"You don't understand. Bunny and I are both going. We enrolled online two days ago. You don't have to pay anything. We're going to West Georgia on financial aid. They're so desperate for students that they'll take anybody right now."

Rochelle searched her eyes and thought that she was telling the truth. "Why now?"

Lacy swallowed hard. "It's not that I didn't want to go to school. I didn't want to leave Bunny. She's the only friend I ever had. She'd been through so much. I couldn't leave her behind. Where would she go if her mama's boyfriend tried to rape her again? All she has is me. I guess it's like how you were with Cotton. I don't know what I would do if something else bad happened to her."

"Is that why you were robbing folks?"

Lacy shrugged. "Kind of. We wanted to get our own place. Now we've got enough money to pay our way through college. We're going to look at a car tomorrow. I wanted to tell you sooner, but I didn't know how."

Rochelle stared at the wall again.

Lacy wrapped her arms around her sister. "I'm sorry about Cotton."

"It's not your fault," Rochelle told her. "Me and Cotton signed our death warrants long ago. I only wanted you to have a different life."

Lacy kissed Rochelle on the cheek. "I will. I promise."

TWENTY SIX

MARCO PULLED UP TO THE DONUT SHOP a little after one in the afternoon. There were a few customers inside, but not many. He spotted Rochelle behind the counter, laughing, and doing her best to please everyone. She squinted out into the parking lot as if she was looking for something or someone. Marco knew that she would not recognize his truck. He'd gotten rid of the Benz. Now he rode in his daily driver, a black Ford F250.

She squinted into the parking lot, then turned back to her customers.

Marco didn't want to go inside. So much had been left unsaid between them. He wanted to admire her from a distance, then pull off and drive far away like the coward he wished he was. But he was no coward.

Marco pulled a facemask over his nose and mouth, then he climbed out of the truck and walked to the donut shop.

Rochelle spotted him through the glass. He could not tell if she was pleased or upset to see him. He tried not to think about it as he walked through the door. She finished serving her customer and turned to him as she stood alone. She asked, "And what can I help you with today?"

He held her gaze and felt his heart turning cold. "Rochelle, we need to talk."

She cocked her head to the side. "You didn't come in here to make a purchase?"

"I just want to talk to you."

"I'm working. I don't have time to talk. And if you're not going to make a purchase, I'm going to have to ask you to leave." She headed down the counter toward the cash register.

Marco smiled. "You got any donuts with Santa faces on them?"

Rochelle stopped in her tracks. She walked back to him. "You're not going to go away, are you?"

"Not unless you tell me too."

Rochelle took a deep breath and let it out. "My best friend was just killed."

"I know. It was my fault." He peered over his shoulder and saw that the customers were wrapped up in their own conversation, yet he leaned over the counter and whispered anyway. "I should have shot Genesis sooner. If I had, Cotton would still be alive."

Rochelle drummed her finger on the countertop. "Blaming yourself is taking the easy way out."

"It's my fault."

"It's not," she said. "You were trying to protect her . . ." Rochelle reached out and laid her hand on top of his. "Like you protected me. If you hadn't told me that Lacy was there, she could have been killed. I loved Cotton, but Lacy . . . that's my sister. I don't know what I would do without her."

Marco didn't know how to respond. He'd lost a brother. Words could not describe the loss he felt. He didn't have to imagine how Rochelle would feel if she had lost Lacy. Which is why he told her in the first place.

"Is your name really Marco?"

He nodded. "Think I lied to you about that?"

"I don't know. You lied about everything else. You didn't tell me you were a cop."

"I *couldn't* tell you that I was a cop. You didn't tell me that you were a robber."

Rochelle reeled back. "What makes you think I'm a robber?"

"I know that was you and Cotton that killed Devon Wright. It was your Maxima. Her BMW. They found blonde hair at the scene. The samples didn't match any DNA database that we have access to, but that's probably because Cotton has never been arrested. But we knew the hair was dyed and originated from a black female."

Rochelle shrugged. "It could have been anybody."

He nodded. "I'll bet the bullets from the Devon Wright crime scene will match the gun Cotton had at Genesis' place. I'll bet a dime to a dollar."

"What do you want me to do, Marco? Admit it? Huh? You gonna arrest me?"

Marco's lips thinned to a line of frustration. "I can't arrest you anymore."

She raised an eyebrow. "Why not?"

"Because I quit. I had to explain my actions this morning. I kept seeing Cotton on the floor, and . . . nobody seemed to give a fuck about her but me. They looked at her as another black stiff in a body bag that they wanted to pin on a black drug dealer. It didn't matter that she had a life, or friends like you, or a future. I—I can't live like that anymore. People matter to me. Being a cop desensitizes you to the point of numbness. You feel nothing. Your only desire is to see people locked up in a fucking cage, and I don't want to live like that anymore."

Rochelle watched him for a moment after he had finished talking. "Where are you going to work?"

"I thought about filling out an application here. Think you could help me get a job?"

She shrugged. "I know a guy." Yet she did not smile.

She asked, "Why did you help me, Marco?"

Marco gestured to the holiday themed cupcakes behind her. "Because it's Christmas."

Rochelle laughed for the first time in two days. She laughed so hard that tears spewed from her eyes, and she could not stop them. She ran around the counter and hugged Marco. He held her close and pulled down his facemask to kiss her cheek. She whispered thank you a thousand times, but her thanks did not replace the pain he felt from watching Cotton die.

"Christmas is over," she said.

"No, it's not," he replied. "Your Christmas has just begun." He pulled her mask down and kissed her lips.

TWENTY SEVEN

WALKING INTO ROCHELLE'S HOUSE was like walking into heaven. There was nothing spectacular about it. He only felt a comfort he had never known before.

They did not stop in the living room. They did not head to the kitchen. Rochelle took him by the hand and led him straight to her bedroom.

She paused in the doorway and embraced him as soon as they stepped inside. She pressed her lips to his.

He broke the kiss. "Your sister. She here?"

Rochelle kissed him again. "I don't care if she is. She might get a little jealous at the noises I'm about to make, but she'll be okay. She's grown. If she wants a man, she knows how to get one. I taught her well."

Marco picked her up and slammed her on the bed. Rochelle shrugged out of her Colorful Confections Donut and Cupcake Shop T-shirt, revealing a plain white bra beneath. Marco unbuttoned her jeans and jerked them down over her hips. Next, he pulled off his own shirt and kicked off his jeans. He climbed into the bed wearing only his boxers and a smile.

Rochelle climbed on top of him and latched onto his neck with all her might. His hands traveled to her wide backside and palmed big handfuls that he didn't want to let go of.

She planted kisses down his chest and belly until she was poised above his boxers. Rochelle stared into his eyes as she pulled them down over his legs and dropped them to the floor. His hard dick stood tall and thick before her eyes. She licked her lips before wrapping her fist around it.

"Rochelle . . ."

"Shut up." She jacked him slowly. "I've been wanting to taste this dick again since that day in the freezer. Don't ruin it. Just lay back and relax." She stared at his penis with wide eyes and kissed the tip.

Marco's mouth yawned open in delight.

Her tongue snaked out and licked his shaft from the base to the top. She opened her mouth and closed it over the head of his dick before he had a chance to catch his breath.

Marco looked down and watched her head bob furiously on his dick as she sucked him. Her fingers fondled his balls, pulling on them gently, until he felt that he was going to explode in her mouth. He sat up and pushed her away. She protested, but he shoved her onto her back and yanked her panties off.

He stared down at her trimmed pussy and his mouth began to water. He pushed her legs wide open and dipped his head low to drink from her fountain. Rochelle gasped when his tongue kissed her clit for the first time. She yanked up the cups of her bra, baring her heavy breasts. Her legs relaxed as she tugged on her nipples while Marco sucked her wet pussy.

"Lick it. Suck my pussy," she purred.

Marco slid two fingers inside her as he ate, working them back and forth to stir her to delight. He looked up and saw her pinching her nipples, head thrown back in pleasure, moaning ferociously. Seeing her like that made him slurp her pussy harder. He wanted to make her cum in his mouth, not because of the sex, but because she needed it.

When he first met Rochelle, he thought of her as a hard-working woman who had been disappointed all her life. An over-looked woman that received no reward for the good things she did. No one ever loved a woman like that. Not because they didn't deserve it, but because she didn't have the time to search for love. Her days were spent working and taking care of home. Love sat on the backburner.

That first look at her from the parking lot of her work did something to him. At that time, he was considering turning in his badge and becoming a full-time hustler. The money was better, and he knew how to get away with it. He had the connects and the knowhow. Making money seemed the only worthwhile endeavor. Chasing criminals that made much more money than him showed Marco that he could have a better life if he switched over to the dark side. Rochelle renewed his faith in humanity. In her, he saw all the goodness of life that money could not bring him. He could buy women. He could not buy love.

Rochelle gripped the back of his head as she came, slamming her pussy into his face. She grinded her clit hard on his tongue and then pulled him up by his chin when she was done.

She kept her legs wide for him to rest there and kissed him tenderly when their lips met. Seconds later, he felt her hands creep between them. Her ass rose from the bed as she slid him inside, with a long drawn-out gasp that escaped with the first feel of his heat filling her up.

Marco needed no convincing. He wrapped his arms around her neck and fucked her slowly until her body relaxed and he could plunge deeper. Rochelle moaned in his ear as he made long strokes that carried his dick out of her, then all the way back in.

He rose up on his hands and looked down as she squeezed her titties together and sucked on her own nipples. The sight drove him crazy.

With her it was much more than sex. Here was a woman that he wanted to love. He wanted to respect her as he had respected his mother. He wanted to give her the life she'd always been missing. The life of love and honor.

Thinking this made his pleasure rise. He clutched her tight.

"Cum inside me," she whispered. "Let me feel it. Please, baby."

Her pussy seemed to get tighter as he fucked her. Her pelvis moved in time with his, meeting him thrust for thrust until they were dirty dancing on the bed. Her arms snaked around his neck and held on tight.

Marco didn't know if she came with him. But he buried himself inside her and let go. All the stress of the last few months escaped with his seed shooting into her. He would still have problems to face in the morning. But for the moment, he was with her, and she took his pains away. That was all that seemed to matter.

When he was done, he remained buried inside her. She held him close and stroked his back while kissing his cheek and whispering, "Thank you."

Marco kissed her ear. "Rochelle, I love you. I know it may be too soon for me to say that, but I feel it."

She was silent for a long time. Finally, she whispered, "I love you too."

EPILOGUE: GENESIS RISING

THE COOK COUNTY SHERIFF'S DEPUTIES arrived at the hospital at six-thirty in the morning. One was a tall white guy with *Bailey* stenciled on his nametag. The other was a stocky Hispanic named Ruiz. They strutted into room 227 carrying leg shackles and handcuffs.

Genesis looked up as the officers entered. He'd just finished breakfast. Scrambled eggs and French Toast. If he had known that he'd be transferred to the county earlier, he would have eaten more. Breakfast in the hospital may have been the last decent meal he would eat for a long time to come.

One morning, days ago, he awoke handcuffed to a hospital bed. His neck throbbed with an intense pain that he'd never felt before. Nurses told him that he'd been shot. It didn't take long for the details of what happened to flood his memory. He saw Cotton's brains splattered on his floor. Hours of lying in a hospital bed allowed him to focus his attention on one name: Mondo.

Detectives came to see him three days after he awoke. They explained that Mondo was actually an undercover cop named Marco. He had infiltrated Genesis' organization and ripped it apart from the inside out. As a result, Genesis had been charged with Cotton's murder and giving the order for his cousin Jamal's killing as well.

How could he have been so stupid? He had yet to view his Motion of Discovery containing the evidence against him, but he knew it all originated with Marco—a cop he allowed into his inner circle. He didn't know exactly what all Marco had told them, but Genesis was hopeful that he could beat the charges. The right lawyer could beat anything as long as he had a fistful of money to grease palms with. And Genesis was lucky enough to have the right lawyer, and the money to pay him.

Bailey stepped close to Genesis and surveyed the blood-stained bandage wrapped around his shoulder and neck. He asked Genesis, "You okay to move? Any strenuous pain we should know about?"

Genesis sat up as far as his handcuffs would allow him to. "You'll have to cuff me in the front."

The cop nodded. "Not a problem."

Ruiz walked over and helped out. They succeeded in securing Genesis in handcuffs and shackles. Minutes later, they led Genesis out of the hospital and to an awaiting squad car. It took some slow movements, but Genesis eased into the back. Despite the physical discomfort, Genesis was eager to get to the county jail. It was a sure sign that things were on the move and almost over.

Ruiz drove. Bailey sat in the passenger seat.

It took five minutes of riding for Genesis to realize something wasn't right. "Officer, isn't the jail the other way? You're driving in the wrong direction."

Neither of the cops said anything. Genesis wasn't a fearful man. In his past, he had looked into the baddest motherfucker's eyes and felt stronger than steel. But sitting in the back of that car made him feel fear in a way he'd never known it before. There was only one man with enough juice to spring him from jail. Hector Guzman.

The squad car pulled behind an abandoned warehouse and parked. Nobody moved. They just waited.

After a few minutes, Bailey asked Ruiz, "You sure your people are going to show up?"

Ruiz kept his eyes looking out of the front windshield. "You'll get your money. Just shut up."

A moment later, a windowless black van crept behind the warehouse and pulled in close to the squad car. Three Mexican men hopped out of the back sliding door.

Ruiz and Bailey stepped out to meet them. As Ruiz spoke to the men, Bailey stood by silently and watched. Genesis said nothing. One of the Mexicans pulled a fat envelop from his pocket and handed it to Ruiz. Bailey came over and opened the back door. He jerked Genesis out.

Ruiz and Bailey worked quickly to remove Genesis' handcuffs and shackles. Once they were free, two of the three

Mexicans grabbed Genesis' arms and held him still. They prodded him toward the van.

Ruiz said, "Wait." When the Mexican men stopped, Ruiz hurried over and spoke in Spanish. One of the men nodded. Ruiz pulled out his service pistol and pressed it against Genesis' palm.

Genesis asked, "What are you doing?"

Ruiz didn't answer him. But as soon as Ruiz snatched his gun back, he spun around and fired, capping Bailey between the eyes.

Genesis reeled back, "What the fuck?"

From there it was a rush to get Genesis into the van. He held out his arms and gripped the door's opening to stay out. There was no way he was getting in that van. If they'd allow a cop to be killed in front of them, what would they do to him? The Mexicans beat his arms with their fists and punched him in the ribs to force him to let go. Honestly, he was too weak to put up much of a resistance. The gunshot wound, plus lying up in the hospital for a few days had him feeling pathetic. He couldn't fight one person, much less the two that held him.

One firm shove got him inside. He rolled onto his back in time to see Ruiz standing beside his squad car, yelling into his radio, "Eighty-one, this is Fifty-seven. Shots fired! Shots fired! Officer down! Need assistance now! Suspect named Genesis Grambling escaped from custody and is armed and dangerous! He is on foot traveling toward Peachtree! Black male! Fifties! Six 'one! Two hundred twenty pounds! Repeat! Suspect is armed and dangerous!" Ruiz turned his pistol to his own shoulder and fired a bullet that ripped into his flesh and smacked the windshield behind him when it came out, shattering the glass.

Genesis gaped in horror just as a black bag was yanked over his head. All faded to black. He tried in vain to make out the shapes in front of him through the porous canvas sack, but all he could see was a shadowed blur with specks of light peeking through.

He heard the van door slam closed. Then the tires squealed on pavement as they sped off.

A heavily accented voice whispered in Genesis' ear, "Mister Guzman has been anxious to speak with you."

www.ingramcontent.com/pod-product-compliance
Lightning Source LLC
Chambersburg PA
CBHW021319190726
48288CB00003B/881